VICTORIA ASHLEY

Hard & Reckless
Copyright © 2017 Victoria Ashley
All rights reserved.

Cover Artist:
CT Cover Creations

Cover Model:
Jonny James

Photographer:
Wander Aguiar

Interior Design & Formatting:
Christine Borgford, Type A Formatting

CHAPTER ONE

Jameson Daniels

WRAPPING AN ARM AROUND MY neck, Katie stands to her tiptoes and presses her lips against mine, before pulling away with a sexy little laugh. "Here you are. Thought you got lost. It's been close to an hour since I've seen you."

Growling, I lift her off her feet, and roughly bite her bottom lip, before moving around to speak against her ear. "I'm always around, baby. Just got a little busy talking about club security. I'll meet you downstairs in a minute. Just need to change first."

With a small moan, Katie releases my neck and slowly runs her hands down my chest and abs, stopping at my belt and tugging on it. "Alright, but hurry. I've been waiting all night to get my greedy little hands on you and have you to myself."

I roughly cup the back of her head, placing my forehead to hers. "Keep talking like that and I'll bend you over the railing right now and fuck you. I don't care that my house is full of people. You know me."

"Mmm . . ." she moans. "Sounds tempting."

"Hey, man. I need you for a minute."

Pulling my forehead away from Katie's, I look over to see Rowdy standing in the hallway with a drink in hand. He's a good friend of mine and another security guard at the nightclub I work at. That's exactly why I like having him around when I decide to throw a party here. More help keeping the people under control when needed. "What's up, Rowdy? Everything okay downstairs?"

He shakes his head. "Nah, I need to talk to you in private. Now."

Katie groans and kisses my cheek. "This is going to be a looong night." Smiling, she gently slaps Rowdy's cheek. "Don't keep my man busy for too long, handsome. I need him if you know what I mean."

Rowdy looks tense, but doesn't say a word as he watches Katie walk away. "Let's go back to the game room," he says stiffly.

He doesn't even wait for me to respond, before he walks away with purpose. Has me thinking that something major is happening.

I don't like that feeling one bit. Has me on edge, ready for something to go down.

Once we get inside the room, I shut the door behind me and walk over to lean against the table. "Alright, well what the hell is going on?"

He runs his ink covered hands down his face and mumbles, making it hard for me to understand what he's saying. "Cole is fucking Katie."

Rage courses through me, causing my blood to boil, as I demand Rowdy to repeat the words that just left his mouth.

I'm hoping like hell that I heard wrong, because I'd hate to have to kill my best friend tonight.

"What the fuck did you just say?"

I grip the table behind me, feeling the veins in my neck begin to throb as I wait for him to speak again. Feels like the longest ten seconds of my life.

"Wait. Shit, I need this first." Holding up his finger, he takes a long swig of his vodka and leans against the wall, before pulling out a joint and lighting it. He takes two quick hits, before blowing out a cloud of smoke. "Cole is *fucking* your girl. They're sneaking around behind your damn back, man." His eyes meet mine, showing me just how gone he is right now. Even high and completely wasted though, he knows that's something you don't fuck around with me about.

"How sure are you?" I growl out, squeezing the table tighter. Something's about to break soon. Probably my damn hand at this rate. "You better be damn fucking sure, Rowdy and not just assuming."

Flexing his jaw, he downs the rest of his drink and then slams the empty glass down next to him, looking pissed that I would even question him. "I wouldn't come to you out of a damn assumption, asshole. I saw the two of them sneak out of the guest room together, looking thoroughly fucked. I wasn't quite as drunk ten minutes ago, but seeing one of my best fucking friends sneak around with my other best friend's girl, had me downing a few shots on the way to find your ass."

Pushing away from the table, I turn around and flip it over, before running my hands over my face and yelling, "Fuuuuck!"

I've never felt so betrayed in my life and there's not a damn word that can explain how I truly feel right now. Over twenty years of friendship with Cole and this is the shit I get. He sleeps with my girlfriend of four fucking years.

"I'd be pissed too, man," Rowdy says from across the room as I pace, trying to gather my thoughts and piece this shit together. "Cole just broke the bro code and in your house to top that shit off. That's messed up. I'd kill him."

My heart is racing so fast that I need to get out of here, before

I explode and take it out on the wrong person. My chest is tight and I can't think straight. None of his words seem to make sense right now. All I feel in this moment is pure hatred.

"Where is he?" I stop pacing to look at him. "Is that piece of shit still downstairs?"

"Nah, man. I saw him walk out the door right when I got up here to find you. He left about five minutes ago."

Cracking my neck, I reach for my jacket and slip it on, before reaching for my helmet. "Watch my house and keep everyone in check until I get back. Don't let anyone upstairs."

"You're gonna chase him down and beat–"

"Damn straight, I am," I say, cutting him off as I rush out the door, headed on a mission. Cole might've left five minutes ago, but I'm faster and more reckless.

"Jameson!" Katie rushes out of the kitchen, grabbing my arm, once I make it downstairs. "Where are you going? Everything okay?"

I yank my arm away, clenching my jaw, as I stop to look at her. She's beautiful as hell, but it's not worth trying to fix this shit. Fuck me over once and you're done. "To find Cole." Feeling my chest ache, I lean in close to speak against her ear. It's the closest I'll ever get to her again. "Get the fuck out of my house. We're done."

The color drains from her face, realization finally kicking in, that I know about her and Cole.

"Jameson, wait!" She attempts to grab my arm again, but I shake it off and push my way through the crowd, needing to get to Cole.

I can hear Katie following behind me, yelling for me to let her explain, but all I see is red as I straddle my Hayabusa and start the engine.

Cole lives less than fifteen minutes from me, so I have about seven minutes to catch him, before he makes it home for the night.

Shoving my helmet on, I rev the engine and speed off, leaving

Katie to scream and cry after me, asking for something that I'll never give her: a second chance.

Leaning forward, I weave my way through traffic, speeding pass vehicles, while on the lookout for Cole's car.

After a while, I spot him two stoplights ahead of me, so I turn off at an alley that I know leads to where Cole is headed.

Speeding up, I fight to control my breathing, but all I can think about is my best friend between my girl's legs, fucking her and making her scream. It only makes it harder to breathe.

Reaching the end of the alley, I turn left, heading toward the side street that I know Cole will be approaching from any second now.

As expected, Cole's black Dodge Challenger, comes into view, making me speed up along the side to pass him.

Pulling out in front of him, once I give myself enough room, my bike skids to a stop, causing Cole to honk the horn and slam on his brakes, almost hitting me.

I don't even care at this point. Him hitting me would only give me more reason to kill his *Don Juan* ass.

After a few seconds, he pushes his door open and steps out of the car, looking me over as if I'm crazy. "What the fuck, Jameson!" He closes the driver door behind him, before throwing his arms up and walking closer to me. "What the hell is your problem? I could've killed your ass. Or shit. Even my damn self. I'm too fuck-ing sexy to die, man," he shouts. "The female population would be left devastated and it would be your fault."

Kicking my stand down, I jump off my bike and pull my hel-met off, tossing it at the road.

That's when I see it register on his face that he knows *exactly* what my problem is.

"Good thing you didn't." Clenching my jaw, I step up in his face and crack my neck, locking my eyes with his dark ones. "Then

I wouldn't get to do this to you for *fucking* my girl."

Swinging out, I punch him in the mouth, causing him to stumble back, before I quickly swing my elbow out, connecting it with his jaw.

This causes him to fall back, but he quickly recovers, jumping back up to his feet and looking me over, with heavy breaths.

His jaw flexes as if he wants to swing back, but he doesn't. Maybe it's because he knows he deserves that and much more.

"Fuck!" Wiping his thumb over his bloody mouth, he cusses to himself, while cracking his neck. "That's some fucked up shit! All over a girl, too? Katie isn't right for you. Never has been. I did you a favor. Open your fucking eyes."

"Fuuck! Always over a girl, Cole." I step up until we're nose to nose, so he can feel my anger with each breath. "Especially when that girl is *mine*. No one fucking touches what is mine."

With that, I grab his throat and squeeze, causing him to growl out as if he wants to rip my throat out just as badly as I want to his. "We've been friends for over twenty years, but fuck me over again and I *will* kill your ass." I slam him down onto the hood of his car and squeeze his neck tighter. "I'll never forget this shit, asshole. This is the worst way to break my fucking trust."

Releasing his neck, I step away from him and bend down to pick up my helmet, before walking back over to hop on my bike. If I have to look at him for another second, I have no idea what I'll end up doing to him.

I hear him coming up behind me as I slip the helmet on and breathe heavily into it. "That's it?" he questions, throwing his arms out and circling around my bike. "We're not going to talk about this shit so I can explain? I wouldn't just fuck your girl without good reason. You know me better than that. You're like a brother to me. Hell . . . you are my brother."

I rev the engine and look him up and down, standing there

with his tattooed fists clenched at his sides. "No, I *thought* I knew you better than that. Your words don't mean shit, so don't bother coming around for a while. This was *nothing* compared to what I really want to do to you. Consider yourself lucky, motherfucker."

Gripping the handle bars, tightly, I take off, finding open road for me to cut loose on, so I can calm down enough, before returning to my party.

I'm usually good at being in control. But not tonight . . . Cole has me all worked up.

This is beyond fucked up on so many levels. Cole's always been the playboy type when it comes to women, but I never in a million years thought he'd pull that shit with my girl.

I thought he knew better than to fuck me over.

I was wrong.

After driving around for thirty minutes, I call Rowdy and tell him I'm on my way and I'll deal with Katie when I get there.

Apparently, after I left, Rowdy tried making her leave, and she got mad, swinging at him.

So, he threw his hands up and backed away, letting her get a few hits to his chest to calm her down.

I'm gonna owe him later for taking a few hits for me.

When I pull up outside my house, Katie is sitting on the porch, but she stands up immediately, when she hears me coming.

The sight of her walking toward me has me tightening my jaw as I take my helmet off, and get off my bike.

"It was just this once, I swear. It'll never happen again. All the other rumors about me aren't true though. You've got to believe me. I'd never hurt you on purpose. I'm just . . . I've been drinking. I wasn't thinking clearly." She grabs my arm and pulls on it, when I just keep on walking. "Will you stop for two fucking seconds and talk to me!"

"Stop with the fucking excuses." Taking a deep breath, I stop walking and look down at her, as she stands in front of me, pushing on my chest to keep me from moving. "Your words mean nothing," I bark. "It's your actions that speak, but you just showed me that trusting you was a mistake."

Her face is red from crying, so I turn away, not letting her tears sway me to change my mind. I know she's not drunk. She might forget how well I fucking know her. She knew perfectly well what she was doing when she went into that room with my best friend.

I *hate* hurting her and seeing her cry, but I stand firm on this shit.

"Jameson, please!" She grabs my face and yanks it so I'm looking down at her again. "Give me a chance to make it up to you. I'll prove to you that I can be trusted. I *love* you. I love you so damn much."

Grabbing the back of her head like I did earlier, I lean in close to her face and stop just inches from her lips. "Goodbye, Katie. Now get the fuck off my property."

With that, I remove her hand from my face and walk inside the house, leaving her outside to let it all sink in.

We're done and there's nothing she can do or say to change that. Just like there's nothing I can say or do to change the fact that she fucked my best friend.

Rowdy meets me at the door with a bottle of Jack, knowing damn well what I need at a time like this.

"Here you go, man. Get fucked up and I'll take care of the party." He grabs my shoulder and squeezes it, as I walk toward the staircase. "You deserve to drown in whiskey so I'll sober my ass up. For you."

Grabbing the bottle from Rowdy, I tilt it back, while making my way up the stairs and to my room.

I'm going to need more than just this bottle to numb the pain I'm feeling right now.

This is going to be a long night . . .

CHAPTER TWO

Two Weeks Later . . .

Jameson

THE CLUB IS PACKED TONIGHT, causing me to keep my guard up and my eyes open for drunken assholes, looking for a fight.

One fuck up and they're out.

Touch any woman in this room wrong or even give them a disrespectful look and I'll be on their ass so fucking fast that they won't even know it until they're out the door, with my knee in their neck.

I'm still on edge over the fact that Cole decided to take his job here back, knowing damn well that I still can't stand the sight of his ass.

I've still been picturing them together, thinking of all the ways I can rip his damn throat out for laying his hands on my girl and touching her in places only I should've been.

That's what him being here does. It allows more scenarios to fuck with my head, intensifying my hate for him.

It's been haunting me, making me want nothing more than to make him feel just a small bit of the pain he fucking made me feel and to let him know what it feels like to be stabbed in the back by the person you trust the most.

I've tried to move on, but I can't. Words can't fix the damage Cole did.

He's across the club, working the back section, but I've had my eye on him, watching him as he flirts with some dark-haired chick.

She's been coming here for the last week since Cole came back, so I can only assume she's here for him.

The animal inside of me, has me wanting to get her alone so I can dig my claws into her and work my way under her skin before Cole gets in too deep with her.

I want to make his ass work for what he wants. He doesn't deserve to have it easy after the shit he pulled on me.

Releasing a frustrated breath, I pull my eyes away from his section of the club and focus back on section A, walking around and making my rounds.

Stopping up at the bar, I tap it to get Violet's attention, noticing that the guy in front of her hasn't given her space since he walked through the door an hour ago. "You good over here, V?"

Looking away from the bearded guy, Violet flashes me a quick smile and leans over to grab my face and press her red lips against my cheek. "I'm always good when your sexy ass is here to keep all the jerks in check. He's a friend, but thank you, Jameson." She makes a sad face and places her hand over mine for comfort, most likely noticing my expression. "Everything okay, honey? I heard about Katie. What a bitch. You're too hot for her anyway, babe. You'll find better."

I tense my jaw and look up at her, trying to keep my cool. "I guess news travels fast around here."

Fucking Rowdy.

"That's what happens when you're friends with Rowdy. He gets high and his sexy lips won't stop moving," she says with a small smile. "But I'm here if you need to talk. I've dated assholes like her before. I know what it takes to get over it and I'm willing to help."

"Thanks, babe." I grab her hand from mine and kiss it, wanting to keep things friendly between us. I have enough messes to clean up at this club. "Let me know if anyone gives you a hard time."

"Will do, babe."

Nodding my head, I leave her alone so I can scan the rest of the room out, keeping my eyes out for anyone who's had too much to drink.

After a while, I get bored, my eyes wandering back over to Cole's section to see that the girl he's been all over is walking through the crowd with one of her friends, heading toward the bathroom.

Cole seems to be busy, so I take this as my opportunity to get her to notice me, making my way through the crowd, ignoring all the other females on the way.

My focus is *her.*

The line to the restroom is long as usual, so she and her friend line up at the end, talking and laughing about something.

The closer I get to her, the more intrigued I become as I step around to the side and my eyes land on her face up close for the first time.

I freeze, unable to turn away as she looks away from her friend to look up at me. She's breathing heavily, fighting to catch her breath from all the dancing they've been doing.

Her long, wavy black hair and bright blue eyes, speak right to my dick, making it stand tall as my eyes roam over her curvy body.

Locking eyes with her, I lift a brow, checking her out, not hiding the fact that I find her attractive.

That's the first step to getting her interested. Curiosity always gets the best of women when it comes to me. Always has.

Tightening my jaw, I allow my eyes to land on her plump lips, before I lick my own and walk away.

I can feel her eyes on me, watching my every step as her friend laughs and tries to get her attention. "Brooke . . . bring it back to reality. You listening to me?"

Satisfied with her reaction to me, I stop Wendy as she walks by, carrying her shot tray. "I'll take those last two shots." I pull out a twenty and drop it on her tray, grabbing the blue shots.

"Sure thing, Jameson." She smiles and holds up the bill with a smirk. "Change?"

"Keep it."

By the time I turn back around, Brooke and her friend are practically standing right beside me now as the line slowly moves up. I can see her secretly checking me out, while her friend continues to talk about Cole, asking her about the sex and how well he can take care of her.

Perfect timing to step in.

Giving them a confident smile, I step into their space, handing them both a shot.

Without giving Brooke the chance to speak, I tangle my hand into the back of her hair and lean in to whisper in her ear, "I'll take care of you. I'm really fucking generous when it comes to women. Just ask my friend Cole." I smile as she leans in closer to my lips as if she wants to hear more. I clearly have her interest now. "Shots are on me."

She lets out a small breath when I pull away, but only offers me a smile as she tilts the shot back, keeping her eyes locked with mine. She seems a bit . . . *speechless.*

I'm still way too close to her personal space, when I look over to see Cole walking toward us.

He doesn't look the least bit pleased as his eyes catch mine, his muscles flexing with each step toward us.

Smirking, I push the ear piece further into my ear, when I hear Rowdy's voice come through, asking me to come watch the entrance door for him. It's a Saturday night so there's no way he'll be able to leave his spot without me filling in for him.

"Great fucking timing," I mumble to Cole, knowing that he can hear Rowdy calling for me.

"You're telling me," he grinds out, getting close to my ear. "Better hurry, Jameson. *I* can take care of my girl just fine. Let's not do this shit. I know where you're taking this."

We both look over to the sound of Brooke's voice. "Jameson . . ." she holds up the empty shot glass and smiles, while looking at my lips as if she wants to taste them. "Thanks for the shot. It was delicious."

"Mmm . . ." her friend wipes her mouth off and smiles up at me, looking satisfied and impressed. "Yes, thank you. It was so good."

"You're welcome, ladies."

Grabbing the back of Cole's head, I get in his face. "Then you know me well. Better hope you can take care of your girl just fine, *brother*. It would *suck* if she decides she wants us both to."

Looking over Cole's shoulder, I wink at Brooke, causing her face to turn red, before she leans in to whisper something in her friend's ear.

Cole's jaw clenches as he watches me grinning like an asshole. "I think she likes me." My smile widens. "I guess we'll just have to see how much."

With that, I walk away, leaving Cole pissed off and probably thinking of all the ways he can keep me away from his girl, now that I've made it clear what's about to go down.

"Jameson, you dick." Rowdy throws the clipboard at my chest, giving me a hard look once I finally make it outside. "Took you long enough."

"Calm the fuck down. It's been five minutes. Your *client* can wait."

"This one doesn't." With that, Rowdy rushes through the parking lot, leaving me to watch the door so he can get high.

Between Cole being here and now dealing with Rowdy's shit, I'm itching to knock someone the fuck out.

I can only hope someone fucks up.

Pulling out a cigarette, I light it and stand back, watching the line full of people, just waiting for a reason to chase someone down.

I need something to get my adrenaline pumping and standing still does nothing but makes me antsy.

Usually, there's at least one idiot who thinks he can sneak his way into the club, without waiting to be let in.

"Jameson," Rev's voice comes through my ear piece, causing me to stand tall and listen. "We have another runner. Left out the back door of the poker room. You're going to love this one." He laughs. "I'm sending Serge to watch the door."

Smirking, I toss my cigarette down, before dropping the clipboard and taking off through the alley.

If it's not someone trying to sneak in, then it's someone trying to sneak out from downstairs.

Adrenaline has me running fast, rounding the corner, just in time to clothesline the idiot, stupid enough to think he can get away without paying his debt.

The guy hits the ground hard, coughing out as his breath gets knocked out of him.

This isn't the first time I've chased him down and I know it won't be the last. He should be banned by now, but I enjoy these moments too much.

Standing over him, I place my foot on his neck and call back to Rev.

"How much does James owe this time?"

Rev laughs into the ear piece. "Damn, that was faster than usual, man. Fifty-five hundred."

Removing my boot from James' neck, I roll him over and pull his wallet from his pocket. "Did you really think it was going to be that easy to get away, James?" I empty the cash from his wallet, tossing the leather down on his chest.

"Yeah . . . thought you were off tonight. Guess I was wrong." He coughs and sits up, watching as I count his money. "I don't have enough cash right now. It's why I ran."

"No shit," I mumble, while grabbing his arm and taking off his watch. "Guess this shit will do."

"It better," he says, while standing up and smoothing out his suit. "That's a Rolex. It's worth way more than I owe."

"Well, consider it a down payment for the next time you run then, asshole." I slap his chest and back up. "Cause we all know I'll catch you again. I'm beginning to like this little relationship we have."

Winking, I turn around and head back to the club, feeling just a tiny bit better now that I've had some action.

Damn, I needed this. I'll have to remember to thank James someday for giving me someone to take my aggression out on . . .

CHAPTER THREE

Brooke Collins

I RELEASE A SMALL BREATH and pull my eyes away from Jameson's firm backside, when Cole grabs my waist and squeezes it, possessively.

"Don't mind Jameson. He's sort of a dick at the moment."

I bring my eyes back to his friend and continue to watch him through the crowd. His body is perfectly sculpted, his hands and knuckles covered in tattoos. He's dressed in a pair of dark jeans and a white button down shirt that shows his back muscles flex with every step he takes toward the exit.

The hat he has on is facing backwards and reads *Security* in bold black letters.

He's completely distracting, even with Cole trying to whisper in my ear and pull me against him.

"Doesn't seem like a dick," I say with a small smile, thankful for his generosity. "He was nice enough to buy us shots that we didn't even ask for."

"That's the problem," he grumbles under his breath.

Curiosity has me wanting to know about this mysterious guy that just seemed to come out of nowhere, looking like pure sex and sin. "How long have you been friends?"

Cole lets out a frustrated breath and pushes his earpiece in his ear, listening to whatever someone is saying in it. "Shit, I have to go downstairs. They need extra security."

Grabbing the back of my head, he crushes his lips to mine, before roughly biting my bottom one. His kiss leaves me speechless and panting against his mouth as he speaks. "If I don't see you again tonight, I'll call you tomorrow when you get off work."

He rushes off, leaving me to stand back and watch his sexy ass as he disappears through the crowd and down the stairs.

I've had a crush on Cole King for a few years now and I just recently got up enough courage to hit on him and give in to my temptation. Hitting on him led to the bedroom and I can't deny that he is hot as hell and extremely talented behind closed doors.

The man uses his body and tongue in ways I've never even imagined were possible and I am far from ready to give that up.

I've heard he's not the relationship type. That he's sort of a playboy, but it won't hurt to stick around for the ride. After the men I've been with . . . hell, I deserve a little fun. Even if it is unattached.

That's exactly what Cole is and his friend looks to be just as fun and tempting as he is.

Karson waits until Cole is out of sight, before nudging me to get my attention. "What was that all about? Did you see the way Cole's friend looked at you and right in front of him too?"

Swallowing, I try to hide my smile, but it's no use. Jameson definitely has my curiosity piqued. "Yeah . . . is it bad that I liked it?"

"Not at all. Two hot friends giving you attention. What's not to like? Think he's outside?" She laughs and grabs my hand, pulling me toward the exit. "But you did start with Cole first, so you should be generous and help a girl out. That is . . . unless they're into sharing. Then I guess you can have both." She lifts her eyebrows, grinning like a maniac. "That would be really hot."

Her words leave me sweating. I've never really thought about having two friends at once, but I definitely am now.

"Tell me about it." I shake my head and follow her through the crowd, looking around for Jameson once we make it out the door.

I can't deny that I sort of hope he *is* outside so I can get another glimpse of him before we leave.

Feeling his eyes on me inside the club was enough to excite me and that hasn't happened in a long time, other than with Cole.

I want to see if seeing him again now, will feel the same way as it did back when we were inside. Maybe it was the adrenaline from dancing that had me all worked up.

I see disappointment wash over Karson's face, once she realizes he must no longer be out here. "That's a shame," she says on a small breath, "I wanted to properly thank him for the shot."

"Maybe next time . . ."

Just as I'm about to look away, my eyes land on Jameson, looking hot and sweaty as he comes from around the corner, smoking a cigarette.

He looks rough as though he's just chased someone down or just had hot, wild sex.

My heart speeds up and excitement courses through me as his eyes seek me out and he flashes me a confident smile, while leaning against the side of the building.

Smiling back, I quickly grab Karson's hand and pull her through the parking lot, knowing that I need to get away now, before I change my mind and want to stay.

I notice an Uber driver, dropping off a few people, so I quicken the pace, pulling her behind me. "I have to work at eight so let's just head out. He must be gone already."

"Ahhh," she groans, while throwing her head back. "It's too early to leave. You're killing my buzz right now."

"Well then, good. Cause it's usually the other way around. Welcome to my world, babe. Doesn't it taste fucking great?"

Muttering, she just hops into the back of the jeep, giving up.

Good . . . cause for some reason, I don't want her getting her hands on Jameson. Not yet . . .

TONIGHT AT *DIAMOND'S* HAS BEEN pure hell and if this asshole in front of me attempts to grab my waist, thigh or ass one more time, he will be eating my shoe, instead of anything on the menu.

My limit is being pushed, and I'm about two seconds away from telling Hal to fuck off and find another waitress for his stupid, poorly ran sports bar.

Not to mention these spandex shorts look utterly ridiculous and spend about eighty percent of the time, riding up my ass.

Kind of like my customers.

I wish more than anything right now that I was still at the club, just dancing and having fun with Karson, instead of dealing with this shit.

Maybe I should've gave in and stayed.

"Listen here, asshole." I slam a pitcher of beer onto the table, splashing it all over my hand. "The only way you'll ever get laid is if you crawl up a chicken's ass and wait. So, touch me again and you'll lose a finger."

The idiot's two friends laugh at the insult, and begin pouring their glasses full of beer again.

They've been here for the last three hours and they're already on their seventh pitcher of beer and apparently, they started to get confident and hallucinate after the fourth one.

"Oh come on, beautiful. Don't pretend you're not going to let me take you home as soon as your shift ends. We both know where this is headed." He smirks and reaches for my waist, gripping it. "I promise you'll have the best night of your life."

"You know . . . it's better to let someone think you're an idiot, than to open your mouth and prove it." Smiling down at him, I grab what's left of the pitcher and slowly pour it over his head. "Now, you might want to go home and take a shower before you get sticky."

"Fucking bitch!" Yelling, he releases his grip on me and stands up, shaking his hair out, before wiping his hand over his face. "Are you insane?"

I slam the empty pitcher into his chest, making him stumble back a bit. "Only when it comes to creeps like you. Learn some damn respect. I'm not here for your touching pleasure."

"Brooke!" I step away from the jerk in front of me and look over to see my boss storming his way over. I haven't seen him look this pissed in a while. "*Please* tell me I'm seeing things and you didn't just pour a pitcher over a customer's head."

Reaching behind me, I undo my money apron and toss it at Hal's oversized head. "You're not seeing things and if you were, then this wouldn't be a damn problem. Learn how to control your customers, before you worry about your staff."

I go to walk away, but Hal grabs my arm, stopping me in place. "Don't walk out, Brooke. You and I both know you're the best I have here. I need you. But I can't have you making a scene every time someone pisses you off."

Narrowing my eyes, I yank my arm out of his grip, tired of dealing with his bullshit. I've put up with it for over two years now and he's yet to get better control over this place. "Oh save your fucking breath. You'll need it to take the rest of the orders tonight."

Everyone in the bar has their eyes on me, watching as I snatch my purse out from behind the register and storm out the door.

Once I step outside, I take a breath and slowly release it, in an attempt to calm down and catch my breath.

I'm so worked up right now, that I'm finding it almost impossible.

Honestly, if I didn't need this shit job to pay my rent and other expenses, I would've left over a year ago. Hal has done nothing but brush off his customers acting badly to keep his business running and them coming back for more.

I can't do it anymore. I won't.

Looks like tomorrow, I'll be on the hunt, but unfortunately, the only experience I have is in waitressing and bartending.

Before my mom passed away twenty-eight months ago, I helped her out at the little café she ran.

I tried keeping it going after she was gone, but I just couldn't. I got depressed and couldn't deal with promoting and finding ways to keep the customers coming in enough to keep the money flowing.

I ended up having to sell it.

After four months of sitting around and grieving, I went to Hal, my mother's old friend, and asked him to give me a job at his bar.

Unfortunately, *Diamond's Bar and Grill*, went downhill just months after I started and Hal became desperate to make money and keep it going.

Good luck to him, because there's no way in hell I'm going back to that shithole.

Walking fast, I reach into my purse and pull out my phone, scrolling through the missed calls and texts.

I smile to myself when I read a text from Cole, asking me if his friend bought me anymore shots after he went downstairs.

His text brings me back to thoughts of the club and it somehow has me smiling and almost forgetting just how pissed off I am right now.

The last few hours have been so busy, that I've barely had time to think and now that I do . . . my mind is on two men.

Two very hot and tempting men that I can't help but want to touch.

Without texting Cole back, I shove my phone back into my purse and begin walking the three blocks to my apartment.

If I text him back, then I know he'll somehow end up in my bed and with how exhausted as I am right now; there's no way I'll be able to keep up with him.

He'll see me tomorrow when I show up at the club, rejuvenated and ready to have a good time.

But for now.

I kick my shoes off and plop down on my bed, knowing *exactly* what will be keeping my mind busy tonight.

I have a feeling it will be a long, hot night . . .

CHAPTER FOUR

Jameson

S ITTING UP OUT OF BED, I reach over for the bottle of whiskey on the bedside table and tilt it back, long and hard, not stopping until my throat burns.

"Fuck," I shake the burn off and set the bottle back down, before throwing the sheet off and getting out of bed.

I have no idea what time it is, but I wish like hell I could sleep the rest of the day away so I wouldn't have to feel shit.

Feeling is all I've been doing lately and I've forgotten just how much it fucking sucks.

Standing still for a minute, I close my eyes and run my hands through my sweaty hair, remembering what it was like to be with Katie.

Yeah, we fought a lot, but it felt damn good to take her to my bed at night, knowing she'd be there when I woke up.

She's the first woman I've allowed myself to get so involved in. The part that gets me the most . . . is Cole knew that shit.

And knowing that he still chose to fuck me over, hurts more than Katie cheating on me.

Taking in a deep breath, I tilt my head up toward the ceiling and slowly release it, before running my hands down my face and walking to the closet.

I pull out a random pair of old jeans and a black t-shirt, making my way down the hall to take a shower.

As the hot water hits my body, I stand here with my eyes open, just staring at the shower wall in a daze.

I feel so fucking out of it. I need something to pull me out of this shit before I lose my mind.

That's where Brooke comes into play.

I remember Cole mentioning her name before in the past. It didn't hit me until late last night, but she's the one he's liked for a while now.

Last time he mentioned her, she was dating some asshole so he just left her alone since she was off limits.

Big fucking surprise there. Katie being off limits didn't seem to do shit to keep his dick in his pants.

"Fuck!" I scream out, while punching the wall. "Fuck this pain."

This shit is killing me and as crappy as it sounds, making him feel just a small portion of what I feel from his betrayal is the only thing that might take the sting away long enough to forgive his ass.

I've already made it my mission to make him work for what he wants. He's going to have to work hard if he wants to keep Brooke to himself.

Call me an asshole, but he knew what he was getting himself into when he decided to stab me in the back.

Stepping out of the shower, I reach for the closest towel and wrap it around my waist, taking a whiff of the air.

"Fucking Rowdy."

I walk down the hall and look over the balcony. As expected,

Rowdy is chillin' on my couch, smoking a blunt.

"What the hell are you doing here so early?"

He looks up at me and smiles, before taking a long hit off his blunt and holding it in while he talks. "It's two. Bout time you got up."

I pull the towel off from around my waist and run it over my wet hair, before replacing it around my waist and making my way downstairs.

Right when I get to the bottom, the doorbell rings. My instincts tell me to let Rowdy handle this.

"I'll be in the kitchen. Get rid of her."

"With pleasure." Rowdy grins, before standing up and walking past me toward the door.

"You just won't give up . . ." I hear him say, on my way to the kitchen.

"Where is he?" she screams. "Jameson—please come talk to me and tell your friend to fuck off."

Rowdy laughs. "He doesn't want to see you. I'm a little surprised you didn't get the hint the first hundred times you showed up at the fucking door."

"Shut up, stoner and move out of my way!" It sounds like Katie is grabbing and slapping at the wall to try to get past Rowdy. "Dammit! Move!"

"Calm the fuck down, floozy."

"Fuck off, Rowdy!"

Finally having enough of her shit, I storm my way into the living room and stop in front of her, punching the door to get the message across.

Her eyes widen and she takes a few steps back, looking surprised. "I just want a chance to explain . . ."

"No," I bark out from the doorway. "I don't want to hear shit coming from your mouth. Rowdy said leave, so bye."

I slam the door in her face and turn around to see Rowdy checking to see if his blunt is still lit.

"Shit. That woman almost knocked the blunt out of my hand."

I'm too worked up to pay attention to what Rowdy says after that.

I need something to calm my nerves and fast, so I snatch the blunt and take off with it up the stairs to get dressed.

"Better not smoke the whole B up there," he yells up at me. "That's the last of my good shit."

I lean over the railing to look down at him, placing it between my lips, before taking a long hit and slowly releasing the smoke.

"Dammit," he complains. "I'll order us some damn pizza then."

"Good idea," I say stiffly.

I sit around in my room for a good twenty minutes, taking swigs of whiskey, before grabbing the clothes I pulled out of the closest earlier.

By the time I get dressed and make my way back downstairs, there's not shit left of his precious B.

I toss the roach at him and he catches it, before placing it in one of his baggies and looking me over as I take a seat next to him on the couch.

"Katie is one crazy bitch, man. She about scratched my eye out, trying to get in. I'm not down with wearing a patch like One-Eyed Willy."

"Sorry about that shit." I stand up, when the doorbell rings, and pull out my wallet for the pizza guy. "Pizza's on me."

I toss a twenty to Rowdy and he rushes over to the door to pay, while I grab for a bottle of vodka and poor him a drink.

I've had enough to drink already and it's barely three in the afternoon so I settle on a water for myself.

As soon as we start eating pizza, I feel Rowdy's eyes on me, watching me as if he's waiting for me to say something.

"Spit it out, Row."

"Not sure I should. Can you handle talking about Cole without choking my ass?"

My jaw clenches at the sound of Cole's name. "I guess we'll see."

Rowdy grabs for his second slice of pizza and sits back, getting comfortable. "Did he have a good reason for fucking you over with Katie? I'd love to hear that shit."

I toss my pizza down and reach for Rowdy's glass. Guess I'll be needing this shit after all.

"Fuck if I know." I down the rest of his vodka and slam the empty glass down on the table. "I haven't given him a chance to explain. Nothing he fucking says can make what he did okay. He fucked everything up the second he stepped into that room upstairs with Katie and sank his dick into her."

When I look back over at Rowdy, he's lighting up a joint this time, lifting a brow as I watch him. "What? You need liquor for this conversation and I need *my* medicine." He offers a crooked smile. "Continue, my friend."

"There's nothing to talk about."

"Is that right?" He laughs. "Is that why he was watching your ass so hard last night at the club?"

I sit up and crack my neck, feeling adrenaline course through my veins when I remember the look on Cole's face when I made it clear he'll be sharing Brooke.

"He had his fun," I say tightly. "Now, it's my turn. What's fair is fair."

"Shit . . ." he takes a hit of his joint and shakes his head. "This should be entertaining to watch. I should probably start to worry."

"Never a dull moment between two best friends pleasuring the same woman. It won't be the first time we've done it. Far from it."

I just hope Brooke can handle what we can bring her . . .

CHAPTER FIVE

Brooke

I SPENT THE WHOLE DAY job searching and ignoring Hal's calls and now I feel extremely tense and in need of some way to unwind and enjoy myself.

The first thing that comes to mind is *Club Reckless*. Cole will be working tonight and so far, his touch has done *wonders* to help me come undone and unwind when needed.

We may have only had sex twice, but that doesn't mean he hasn't done other things to get my body heated and begging for more. The man can work wonders with his fingers.

Now, just the sight of him somehow gets my body hot and that's what I need before I go crazy from this stress.

I'm just getting out of the shower and getting ready to call Karson, when a text comes through from Cole.

My heart jumps round in my chest as I open his message and read it.

Cole: I'm coming by after work tonight. I need to fucking taste you.

"Holy hell," I breathe out, while slipping into my new black dress. "This man and his dirty mouth."

Pulling my bottom lip between my teeth, I lay back on my bed and smile, trying to decide if I want to let him know I'm coming to see him at the club or just surprise him.

Me: Is that right? Where do you want to taste me?

Cole: Fuuck . . . my dick is so hard right now even thinking about where. I'm stroking myself.

Me: Show me . . .

My whole body heats up as a picture of him holding his dick for me comes through. It's so damn big and hard.

Knowing he's thinking about me, while stroking himself, has me completely turned on and reaching down to get ready to touch myself.

Right as I slip my hand under my panties, the front door opens, causing me to pull my dress back down and slam my face into my pillow.

"Where you at?" Karson yells from the hallway. "You ready yet? The cars running."

I hear her laugh as she walks into my room and sees me grunting into my pillow, while wrapping it around my face.

"Bad timing?" she questions. "You really need to work on that."

I nod my head and roll over, running my hands through my hair, sexually frustrated. "Very . . . and I think it's you that needs to work on that. You're the worst friend ever."

Walking over to my bed, Karson reaches for my phone and unlocks the screen. Her eyes widen when she takes in the picture I never closed.

"No wonder you've had a crush on him for so long. Holy sex

god . . . that is a nice penis."

Rolling my eyes, I sit up and snatch my phone out of her hand, before crawling out of bed and slipping into a pair of black heels.

"Yeah, and you just ruined the fun I was about to have with it. So . . . thanks for showing up early."

"Oh, stop complaining. We're heading out to see him now. Maybe you can pull him into the bathroom and have fun with the real thing. That sounds soooo much better than pleasuring yourself to a picture of it. We're not in high school anymore."

Her words have me smiling as I picture just that. I've never had sex in a public place before and I can't deny that I've dreamt of it many, many times before.

"See?" She grins and watches me bite my lip in thought. "Sounds so much better, right?"

Releasing a breath, I reach for my purse and grab my wallet out. "Let's get out of here. It's been a long, shitty day and I need to go have some fun."

She heads for the door, motioning for me to walk out first. "I hear ya, babe. I've been ready."

My thoughts take over on the drive there and before I know it, I'm wondering about Jameson and if he'll notice us here tonight.

As much as I've tried not to think about him, I can't help but to be a bit curious.

"Maybe his hot friend will be working tonight too," Karson says as we pull into the parking lot, searching for an empty space. "I had naughty dreams about that man last night. Did you get a look at that firm ass?"

Ohhh did I ever . . .

"Maybe . . ." I grab her arm and smile at the cute security guard at the door as we approach him. He's the same one that let us in last night.

Except this time, he doesn't even check the list to see if we're on it, he just flashes us a sexy smile and checks off something on his list.

Rowdy his black t-shirt reads. He's tall and fit, his neck and arms covered with tattoos.

He brings his hand up, running it through his wild, messy hair, before speaking. "Hope you ladies enjoy yourselves tonight. Find me if you don't." He winks at Karson and checks her out in her skinny jeans and heels as she reaches for money to pay the entrance fee. "Jameson has you both covered tonight. Go on in."

His blue eyes are bloodshot as he looks us over and waves his arm, allowing us to pass.

"Thanks, gorgeous." Karson bites her bottom lip, while looking him over and shoving her money back into her jeans. "Stop over and say hi if you get a break, yeah."

Rowdy crosses his toned arms and stands back, smiling at us as we pass him to enter the club.

I shake my head and laugh as we head over to order drinks. "You really think he'll be able to find you in this crowd?" I ask over the music. "I have a hard-enough time finding Cole and he has a shirt with the club logo on the back."

She shrugs and gets the bartender's attention, ordering us both a mixed drink. "I guess we'll see."

An hour into being here and I have yet to find Cole anywhere. So, I continue to dance, while occasionally looking around me, in hopes he'll pop up.

I'm half tempted to say screw surprising him and just text him to ask where he's at in this crazy place, when I suddenly feel a firm body, slip in behind me and wrap an arm around my waist.

The way Cole grinds his body against mine, while burying his face into my neck, has me leaning into his touch and moaning out.

Everything in the way he moves and touches me is so damn sexual and erotic and I'm so close to the edge that all I want to do is reach behind me and grab him.

After seeing it in a text, I *need* to feel him in my hands.

Softly moaning, I slide my hand in between our bodies and run it over his hard dick. It feels so damn big in my small hand. "I've been looking everywhere for you," I breathe out, as his lips gently caress my neck.

"I don't think I'm the man you're looking for . . ." a deep voice that *isn't* Cole's says against my ear. "But I promise you I'm just as good. I can prove it," he whispers the last part, sending chills over my body.

Sucking in a surprised breath, I remove my hand from his dick and turn around. My heart about flies out of my chest, when my eyes land on Jameson.

He doesn't look the least bit upset that I was just groping his dick as if I own it, but me . . . I feel like an idiot right now. A huge one.

How embarrassing.

Smirking, Jameson looks down at me, while running one of his tattooed hands down my neck, before grabbing it and leaning in to speak. "Sorry for intruding, but you looked so fucking sexy from across the room . . . I couldn't resist touching you."

I swallow and lock eyes with him, feeling heat shoot throughout my whole body as his thumb runs down the front of my neck. "Uh . . ." I smile and release a small breath, feeling weak under his touch. "Shouldn't I be the one apologizing?"

His thumb moves up to brush over my bottom lip, as he steps in closer to me, until our bodies are molded together. "Never apologize for getting me hard, Brooke."

The sound of Karson's voice has me breaking eye contact with Jameson. "Woah! I turn my back for a few seconds and turn back to find you getting it on with Cole's friend." She smiles. "Thanks for paying our way in, by the way."

Jameson smiles, but keeps his eyes on me. "Anytime."

I find myself swallowing again as I look up to make eye contact. "Yes . . . thank you."

He does this little half smirk that has my body aching to pull his bottom lip into my mouth and suck it.

Having him so close, almost makes me forget I came here in search of Cole to begin with.

He could be anywhere in this room, yet Jameson doesn't seem to care that our bodies are practically on top of each other's.

Maybe they really *are* into sharing.

The thought has me breaking a sweat and waving my hand in front of my face to cool off.

"You okay?" Jameson questions, his face growing serious. "Need me to back up? I know my body can make it a little *hot*."

"You're good," I whisper. "*Really* good."

I didn't think he'd be able hear that over the music, but from the cocky look on his face right now, I'd say he's good at reading lips.

"Where's Cole?" Karson asks from beside us with a grin. "Shouldn't *he* be the one over here dancing all over Brooke?"

"He's downstairs," he answers. "That's why I'm keeping her company. Being a good friend and all."

Karson shakes her head and laughs, before turning around and dancing with some random guy that shows up.

This has Jameson leaning down to place his forehead to mine, while running his hands down the side of my face.

While, I'm standing here breathing heavily from his closeness, he grips my hips with both hands and guides his leg between mine, before grinding his body against mine to the music.

Getting lost in the moment, I wrap my arm around his neck and move my hips with his, exhaling as I feel his erection pressing against me.

With control, he spins me around in his arms, grabbing me

from behind, his body grinding with perfection against my ass.

I lean my head back and moan, when I feel his hand run down the front of my body, before moving around the side to dig into my thigh.

"I'm so fucking hard," he whispers against my ear. "You have no idea how easy it would be for me to lift your dress right here and prove to you I'm just as good as my friend."

I feel my body clench from his words.

"It's dark, Brooke and dancing is so close to fucking." He runs his hand over my arm, before kissing my neck, sending chills over my body. "Want to test it out?"

"Jameson . . ." I close my eyes and moan out as his hand brushes over my ass. There's something about the way he touches, that makes a girl weak. "Are you always this tempting?"

"Yes," he breathes.

I about die when I hear someone speak into his earpiece. "You're on your button, Jameson. Stop fucking around and get back over here."

Growling, he releases his grip on me and fixes his earpiece, before saying something back that I can't quite hear.

When he's done, he steps around me and pulls out his phone. "What's your number? You can text me if you need anything."

Without hesitation, I give him my number and watch as he hits the numbers in.

Smirking, he drops his phone back into his pocket and looks me over, while backing away.

"I'll see you around."

"Yeah," I breathe out. "See you around . . ."

My heart is about beating out of my chest, by the time he disappears through the crowd.

Holy hell. Now, I really need to take care of myself . . .

CHAPTER SIX

Jameson

C ALL ME AN ASSHOLE, BUT I knew Cole would be listening from downstairs, too busy and unable to get free from the poker room.

He's probably fuming right now, thinking of all the ways he can pleasure her better than me to make sure she continues to want him more than she wants me.

Being on the dancefloor with her, feeling the way her body reacted to mine, just proved to me that I've got her interest for sure now.

Now, I need to figure out what to do with it.

Her body is so wound tight, just begging for release and I want to be the one to give it to her before Cole can.

Lucky for me, tonight is my night off, so I'm only here for coverage for a couple hours.

As soon as Rev gets back from his break, I have to send Rowdy on his and then I'm free for the night.

Cole can't say the same for another two hours. What an unfortunate son of a bitch.

My plan is to take it slow on Brooke and work her body up so much, that she not only wants me to fuck her, but *needs* me to.

I don't mind sharing Cole's girl with him. That way he gets to *see* and *hear* just how much she enjoys riding my cock.

Then after that, I'll back off and let him have his girl. I'll call it even and we'll move the hell on.

Taking over for Rev, I stand back in section B and watch as Brooke and her friend dance, just enjoying themselves.

The sexual frustration on her face as she sips her drink, leaves me grinning like a fool, knowing that her need for release is partly due to my little visit to the dancefloor.

Truthfully, I would've fucked her right there on the spot if I was a bigger asshole. My dick was painfully hard, straining to break free from my pants.

But I know working her up slowly will ensure she wants me for longer. Which means longer suffering for Cole.

A few small distractions pull my attention away from Brooke as I make my presence known to a couple assholes that are beginning to get rowdy.

"Break one more fucking bottle and I'll break your face on the floor and then make your friend clean it up. Got it?"

The guy whose shirt I'm gripping, nods his head and throws his arms up. "Got it. Sorry, man. Was just having fun."

I release the douche's shirt and shove him toward the broken glass. "Make sure you get every last shard. You and your asshole friend."

The guys face turns red with embarrassment as the girl he's with stands back and watches him bend down to clean up the mess like a little bitch.

That's what happens when you party like an asshole.

By the time Rev comes back over to take over his section, I no longer see Brooke or her friend on the floor.

"Thanks, man." Rev smiles and takes a drink out of his water bottle, before crossing his arms. "Who was that beautiful woman you were dancing with before I interrupted your ass?"

I flash him a crooked smile. "Cole's girl."

"Ah shit." He shakes his head, while replacing his earpiece. "I'm staying far away from that shit. There's bad news written all over it."

"Maybe . . ." I look around to see if I can find Brooke, but they're still lost in the crowd somewhere. "I guess we'll see."

With that, I make my way through the crowd and outside to relieve Rowdy from door duty for his twenty-minute break.

"About time, brother. I have someone to find." He winks and takes off in a hurry, wasting no time disappearing inside.

Usually, he spends his breaks out back, smoking a joint. Looks like there's something he wants more tonight.

He's not the only one.

Pulling out my phone, I find Brooke's number and send her a text, knowing it'll leave her thinking about me.

Jameson: I'm getting off in twenty. Look for my text later.

Twenty minutes goes by without a response from her, so I'm guessing she's still here. There's no way she had a phone hiding anywhere in that tight little dress of hers.

Rowdy shows up to take back over, sweaty and out of breath.

"Enjoy your break?"

He smiles and fixes the buttons on his shirt. "I think Karson did."

"Is that right?" I laugh as he reaches down to adjust his erection. "I'm guessing you didn't relieve that shit in the corner somewhere?"

"Nah." He runs his hands through his sweaty hair and fixes the ring in his nose. "Her hands were all over my body though. Fuck she's fast at touching what she wants." He makes a pained face and growls under his breath. "Cole's girl was looking a little lonely in there. Hot and lonely. You going to go show her a good time?"

"Nah . . ." I slap the back of his head and smile, while pulling out my earpiece. "See ya later, man."

I *could* go back in and find Brooke before I leave, to give her another little taste of the things I want to do to her, but I have something else planned for tonight. A little show I know she won't be able to forget.

Tonight, is just the beginning . . .

CHAPTER SEVEN

Brooke

S WEATY AND OUT OF BREATH, I grab Karson by the arm and pull her through the crowded club, just needing to break free so I can breathe for a moment.

Bodies are so piled up on the dancefloor that I seriously feel as if I'm suffocating. Not to mention my feet are killing me and if I don't sit down soon and give these heels a break, I might just scream.

I'm thinking maybe it's just time to call it a night and wait to see Cole when he gets off work tonight.

"Done already?" Karson whines, while stopping me from pulling her. "I need water before we leave. This way."

With force, she tugs me the opposite direction, leading us toward the bar. Once we reach it, she shoves her way between two guys to catch the bartender's attention.

As she's splashing water all over herself and making these strange noises that I choose to pretend I'm imagining, I look over and spot Jameson standing off to the side, talking to some silver fox in a nice suit.

Maybe the owner or manager.

Jameson looks as if he's about to leave for the night.

His eyes meet mine for a split second and a small smile takes over, making him look seriously irresistible.

I feel my body just screaming out for him, wanting to feel him under my hands.

"Much better," Karson says, bringing my attention back to her. "Now, we can go."

By the time I look back over, Jameson is gone, so I allow Karson to pull me along with her toward the other side of the room.

Just as we're about to reach the exit door, Cole comes walking toward us, looking extremely sexy and edgy as he looks me over as if he wants to bite me and leave his mark.

His white button down is clinging to his chest with sweat, and the top two buttons are undone, revealing his neck tattoos.

Without a word, he grabs me and slams me against the wall, before wrapping my legs around his waist and sucking my bottom lip into his mouth.

Grabbing onto his hair for support, I moan out against his lips before grinding my hips into him. "Cole . . . I've been waiting to see you."

"Fuck . . . Brooke," he growls. "I've been wanting to do this for hours." He bites my lip and cups my ass in his hands. "I have less than two hours before I'm off. I'll just meet you at your house around two."

I release a breath and my whole body shakes as he digs his erection between my legs, making it clear what he wants from me.

If it weren't for the fact it's so dark in this corner, people would think we were having sex right now.

"You're rougher than usual," I whisper into his ear. "I like it.

It's hot."

"Good. I have reason to be." He runs his lips up my neck, stopping below my ear. "Be ready for me."

Releasing my legs, he looks me in the eyes, while moving his hands up to grab my face. "I can be as rough as you want, baby. We're just getting started."

"We?" I question, feeling a bit breathless.

Before he can respond, Karson clears her throat from beside us. "You know . . . I'm still here. And so are hundreds of other horny people. Maybe you should save this for later."

Smiling, Cole backs away from me, looking my body over, before he speaks. "So damn beautiful. Keep that dress on so I can tear it open with my teeth later."

Holy shit!

He disappears through the crowd, leaving me panting against the wall, unsure of what to do with myself now.

My whole body is on fire.

Looking speechless, Karson begins walking me outside as if I need an escape and fast. "We need to get you home before your vagina explodes. I don't know what you have going on with these two boys, but I would give *anything* to trade places with you right now."

"I don't know," I say heavily as we step outside. "I must've done something fantastic to deserve this."

"You're telling me. When you find out what, I want to know." Smiling, she turns around and blows a kiss at Rowdy, before spinning back to face me. "Let's go before I decide I need a drink."

Once we get inside her vehicle, I grab my wallet and phone out of her glove compartment and scroll through my missed texts.

One came through about twenty minutes ago, from a number I don't recognize.

Unknown: I'm getting off in twenty. Look for my text later.

My whole body tingles as I read over the message for a second time.

It has to be from Jameson. Who else would it be?

"You okay over there?" Karson pulls out of the parking lot and starts heading toward my apartment. "You look a little squirmy over there and your fingers are digging into your dress."

"I'm fine," I answer quickly, while releasing my grip on my dress. "Just hurry and get me home so I can bury my face back in my pillow and scream."

"Ahhh . . ." she laughs. "Which one are you gonna imagine first tonight? Cole or his friend? That's a tough choice."

"None of your business." I laugh. "Just step on it."

I keep my phone in my lap the whole way home, looking down every few seconds, waiting on another text from Jameson.

My heart is pounding, going crazy with anticipation to see what he's going to send me next.

I have no clue what I'm doing or what these boys have planned for me, but I can't seem to stop wanting them both right now.

Clearly, they both know what they're doing.

Do I just go along with it?

My phone goes off in my lap, interrupting my thoughts.

I'm a little too quick at unlocking my phone and diving face first into the screen, that it has Karson side eyeing me as I read the message.

Jameson: Your body seemed so tense and sexually frustrated on the dancefloor. Cole not taking care of you like he should be?

My face turns red from his question. Was it that obvious I'm extremely in need of an orgasm right now? And how the hell do I answer that?

Me: He sent me a little treat earlier on his way to work.

Jameson: I'm extremely generous with treats myself. I'd like to think a little more so than my friend . . .

Jameson: A dick pic?

"What's going on over there?" Karson questions, while trying to peek over at my phone. "Who are you texting?"

A rush of excitement washes through me as I say his name out loud. "Jameson."

"Well, he sure didn't waste any time. He moves fast!" She pulls up outside my apartment building and smiles over at me as I reach for the door handle. "You're just going to leave me with that?"

I open the door and laugh. "That was my plan."

"You suck," she grunts and waves me away. "*Enjoy* your night, babe. I'll call you tomorrow after I get off work."

Stepping out of her car, I shut the door behind me and text Jameson back.

Me: Lucky guess on the dick pic?

Jameson: I know Cole . . .

Jameson: But like I said . . . I'm a little more generous. Tell me where you live.

I'm just about to open the door to the building, but stop as I read his last text.

He wants to know where I live.

"Shit . . . shit . . . shit. What do I do?"

I try to convince myself it's a bad idea to tell Jameson where I live, but I can't stop my fingers from sending him my address.

Releasing a hard breath, I walk with shaky legs to the elevator, stepping inside as someone gets out.

I ride it up to the third floor and rush into my apartment, slamming the door shut behind me.

"Maybe he won't really show up," I tell myself, while tossing my wallet down and beginning to panic. "I mean . . . who just does that?"

I stop pacing and look down at my phone when it goes off in my hand a few minutes later. I expect it to be Jameson, but it's Cole's name that pops up on the screen, causing me to lose it this time.

> *Cole: I haven't been able to stop thinking about fucking you since I slammed you against the wall.*

> *Cole: Leave your door unlocked.*

As soon as I finish reading Cole's text, the doorbell rings. *Oh. My. God . . .*

CHAPTER EIGHT

Jameson

A PPARENTLY, MY FRIEND COLE IS still a fucking amateur when it comes to giving women a damn treat.

I don't even remember the last time I sent a girl a picture of my dick. I like to share the *real* thing. It's so much better in person.

That's exactly what a woman as beautiful as Brooke deserves. She wants a treat . . . I'll give her one she won't stop thinking about for weeks.

A little something to remember me by as Cole sinks into her later. When he makes her scream, it'll be for both of us.

Standing tall, I ring the doorbell, feeling the excitement start to kick in at what I'm about to do.

Is it bad it has me more turned on than usual, just knowing it's Cole's girl I'm about to do this for?

Fuck it. I don't feel one ounce of guilt. Not after what he did to me and maybe he should've thought it through before sending a lame as picture.

He should already know I'm going to go out of my way to top that shit.

The door opens to Brooke standing there, shoeless, still wearing her tight little dress. The black fabric is molding to her every curve, making me want to bite her in places that'll have her screaming.

She looks excited, yet nervous as she looks me over and steps aside, allowing me to walk inside.

"Can I get you a drink?" She offers, while trying her hardest not to let her eyes wander down to where I know she wants to look the most. "I have some Jack in the kitchen."

"Absolutely. One thing you'll learn about me is I can never say no to Jack." I follow her into the kitchen and step up behind her, reaching up to grab two glasses out of the cupboard, before she gets the chance to. "The other thing you'll learn is I can never pass up the opportunity to give a beautiful woman the best orgasm of her life." I smile against her ear. "You'll definitely need a drink for this."

I hear her breath slowly escape her as I set the glasses down on the counter and run my thumb up the side of her neck. "I don't even have to *touch* you yet, babe. We can save that for next time."

"Holy shit," she whispers, while pointing to another cupboard. "The Jack's up there."

Smirking, I walk over and grab the bottle down, watching her watch me as I pour us both a glass.

"You're pretty good at this, I take it."

I grip her waist with one hand and lean in to speak against her ear. "What's that?"

"Working a woman up so tight that she feels as if she's about to explode from sexual frustration."

"I am."

Releasing the grip on her waist, I walk into the living room and take a seat on her leather recliner, making myself comfortable.

Leaning back, I bring my glass to my lips and take a swig of whiskey, my eyes following Brooke as she takes a seat on her couch and crosses her legs.

I can tell her pussy is sensitive from the way she squirms with each movement she makes.

The room is already dim, which makes this the perfect mood to get this started, before Cole gets off work.

I just hope she's ready for this . . .

Brooke

STEELING HIS JAW, JAMESON STANDS up and slowly unbuttons his white shirt, keeping his amber eyes on me as I watch him, my chest moving faster with each button he undoes.

The firmness of his tattooed chest has me going crazy inside to touch him. I want nothing more than to run my fingers over every ridge of muscle and feel him.

When he gets to the last button, he pulls the fabric back, giving me a perfect view of his *perfect* body.

I can barely catch my breath as I watch, waiting to see what he'll do next.

Reaching for his glass, he tilts it back, looking so damn sexy, as he stands there with his chest and abs bared to me. His tight muscles flex with each move he makes as he takes a seat again.

Not knowing what to say, I slam my glass back, emptying it half-way. The liquid burns my throat, but gives me the small distraction I need right now.

Looks like he was right about me needing this drink.

Knowing I'm watching his every move, he roughly runs his

hand through his dark hair, while moving the other one down his body, stopping on his belt.

My insides do flips as he yanks on the belt before undoing it and then undoing the button on his pants.

He's working slow, most likely knowing he's working my body up with the anticipation of how far he plans on taking this.

Surely, he's not just going to whip his dick out and stroke it for me. *Is he?*

I swallow at the thought and rub my thighs together, softly moaning from the sensation. I'm so damn sensitive right now that I'm afraid any movement might set me off.

Breathing heavily, I grip onto the couch and dig my nails in when I hear Jameson's zipper next.

It seems so loud in the otherwise silence of the room. It's as if it's taunting me with its sound.

"Jameson . . ." I breathe out. "Does Cole know you're here?"

He gives me a crooked smile and lowers the top of his pants, before running his palm over his erection and moaning. "He will . . ."

I really should be questioning this more right now, but my mind can't focus. Jameson's body is enough to make a girl go stupid with need.

My eyes seem to be glued to his strong hand as it continues to stroke his dick through the blue fabric of his boxer briefs.

I know from my little experience earlier just how big it is and I can't deny I wish I could touch it just like I did back at the club.

"Want to see me come, Brooke?" he asks in a husky voice, while squeezing his dick. "I can finish what Cole started. No touching required."

Holy shit . . . holy shit.

I find myself nodding. It's as if he has some kind of control over my body, just by touching his own.

My heart is beating so damn hard at the moment that I feel

as if it's about to burst through my chest as he slowly lowers his briefs, exposing the flesh of his extremely hard dick.

We both moan out as he strokes it a few times with one hand, before grabbing it with both, while leaning his head back into the leather.

"Be strong," he growls out. "One touch and you'll come for me. You want it to be when I do. Trust me."

I feel myself beginning to clench with each stroke of his perfect dick. I'm so close to the edge that I'm not sure I can hold back until he's done.

His deep moan has me digging my nails deeper into the couch, fighting to hold on for as long as I can.

"I can't," I pant out. "I need to come right now, Jameson."

"Fuuuuck . . ." he digs his teeth into his bottom lip, while standing to his feet, giving me a better view of him stroking himself.

His eyes close and he leans his head back, growling with each hard stroke of his dick.

He's like a masterpiece standing before me, his body so perfectly sculpted and his deep moans like music to my fucking ears.

How the hell can someone make me feel like this? How can someone make me want to come undone without a single touch.

I'm so close . . . so fucking close.

"Now," he orders. "Touch yourself."

Not able to hold back any longer, I slip my hand under my dress and run my thumb over my clit, losing it with one single touch, as Jameson growls out, catching his own release in his palm.

Seeing his come coat his hand has me losing it harder than I ever have before.

It's so fucking hot.

I close my eyes and lean my head into the leather couch, while fighting to catch my breath.

I can't believe that just happened.

Now, I'm sitting here with soaked panties, my pussy throbbing so hard that I know I won't be able to walk without crying out from the sensitivity.

When I open my eyes again, Jameson is watching me with a confident smirk, while using his shirt to clean his hands off.

"Cole should be on his way over," he says stiffly. "I should get going."

Reaching over, he drinks the rest of his whiskey, before setting the empty glass back down on the table.

Then he walks over to me, spreads my legs and slowly runs his fingers over my wet panties. "Fucking perfect," he whispers. "That'll save Cole the work of getting you ready for him."

My eyes move away from his hard chest to meet his gaze. "You're leaving?" I question between breaths. "Not going to wait for your friend?"

His jaw muscles flex as he looks me over. "It's too soon for that. But I'm up for sharing the next time I visit. As long as Cole can handle it."

I release a slow breath and smile, wanting that more than anything. Something inside tells me I won't be completely satisfied until I have them both at the same time now. "Let's hope he can then," I say through heavy pants.

With that, he leans in and places a kiss to the side of my mouth, letting his soft lips linger for a few seconds. "Goodnight."

"Goodnight," I whisper, unable to believe what just happened.

A few seconds later, the door opens and closes, letting me know he's gone.

"What the hell just happened?" I whisper to myself, breathless.

I find myself looking up at the clock to see that it's now just a little past two.

Cole should be here any second now.

And as bad as it sounds, I need him inside me and fast. I want to pull his hair as he pounds into me, taking me hard and fast.

As much as Jameson satisfied me with his dirty little show, there's no way any woman can witness that and *not* want to have rough, dirty sex afterward.

Just as I'm finally catching my breath, the door opens and Cole steps in, looking powerful and on edge.

His eyes land to me on the couch and he must be able to tell how worked up I am, because he doesn't waste any time coming at me.

He's so damn sexy right now, breathing heavily as he picks me up to my feet and yanks my dress off over my head.

Without a word, he places his hand between my legs and slowly runs his fingers over my wet pussy. "I saw Jameson on the way in," he says tightly. "Did he fuck you?"

I shake my head, before moaning out as his thumb brushes over my sensitive clit.

"Good."

Ripping the buttons of his shirt open, he yanks his shirt off, revealing his firm chest, before undoing his pants and kicking them to the side.

With heated eyes, he steps toward me, gripping my face roughly, before crushing his lips to mine and biting me so hard that he almost draws blood.

That one kiss feels so much rougher and deeper than the rest. As if he has something to prove.

With his lips still on mine, he yanks my bra off, before slipping his hand into my panties and burying two of his fingers inside of me.

I can hear just how wet Jameson left me as Cole pumps in and out of me.

I can tell he notices too, because he lets out a frustrated breath, before picking me up and carrying me to my room. Once we get close enough to the bed, he roughly tosses me onto it.

My breath gets knocked out of me for a quick second, but that quickly doesn't matter anymore as I lay back and watch him step out of his black boxer briefs.

He's hard and I can see the bead of moisture on the head of his dick, before he wipes his thumb over it.

"Better hold onto the mattress, babe. This might get a little fucking rough."

Walking over to the side of my bed, he reaches into my nightstand and pulls out a condom, ripping it open with his teeth, before rolling it on.

My body is aching so damn bad to have him inside of me that I'm not sure if I should be aggravated with Jameson or thankful.

Cole has always turned me on, but with just seeing Jameson touch himself for me, everything seems to be intensified at the moment. They're the perfect team to make a girl go crazy with need.

With force, Cole grabs me and flips me over, grabbing the back of my neck as he yanks my panties down and slaps my ass.

He slaps it one more time with a growl, before rubbing his erection over my entrance and then pushing inside of me.

I cry out from the intrusion and grip the blanket as I scream. "Cole!"

"Scream my name again." He pulls out of me and slams back inside, making me scream. "Louder this time. I want the neighbors to hear it."

He rams into me so hard that I scream out, and grip the blankets tighter. "Cole! Fuck . . . oh fuck . . ."

He wraps his hand into my hair and pulls my head back, digging his teeth into my neck as he continues to thrust inside of me.

Within a few minutes, I cry out from my orgasm, digging my nails into Cole's arm as I come around his dick.

"That's it," he growls against my ear. "I love it when your pussy clenches around my dick. So fucking tight."

Wrapping one of his arms around my neck, he grabs my breasts with his other and pounds into me so fast and hard that I bounce up with each thrust, it hurting as I come back down, our bodies slapping together.

After about twenty more minutes of one of the best fucks of my life, Cole bites my shoulder, growling out as he comes inside the condom.

I can feel it filling the condom and this leads me to coming again, imagining the both of them filling me.

This is dirty . . .

Yet so fucking exciting.

I need to have these boys at the same time.

My body won't be completely satisfied until I do . . .

CHAPTER NINE

Jameson

I DIDN'T SLEEP FOR SHIT last night. Not even a bottle of whiskey was enough to calm my fucking racing mind.

Between my phone going off with numerous texts from Katie begging me to see her, I couldn't get the look on Brooke's face when I made her come leave my mind.

She was so damn beautiful coming undone for me, that I can't stop myself from wanting to make it happen again.

Her lust filled eyes gave her away.

I'm getting under her skin and leaving my mark. I have no doubt after last night I've made her want me sexually *almost* as much as she want's Cole.

I was hoping last night would make me feel somewhat better about Cole fucking me over, but I'm not even close to being over wanting to choke him yet.

Yeah . . . I made his girl come for me, but I haven't even touched her yet. She hasn't felt what it's like to have me inside of her.

Katie felt what it was like to have Cole, now Brooke has to feel what it's like to have me. This is the *only* way for me to move past this.

It's going to piss Cole off in the process, but in the end, I'm hoping it's enough to let me forgive my best friend and move on.

Twenty years of friendship is worth a lot to me. Cole is my family and *this* will tell me if it's worth just as much to him.

He knows me. He knows I have to do this shit and he knew it the second he made his decision to fuck my girl.

From the look Cole gave me when we passed each other in the hallway of Brooke's apartment last night; I think he knows just as well as I do how this is all going to play out.

He's going to play along for a bit, while secretly stabbing me in his fucking mind, wanting to kill my ass for putting him through this.

The fucker's sorry for what he did, even if he *did* have a good reason like he said.

That's exactly why he hasn't come to my doorstep to choke my ass out for last night yet.

And within the next thirty minutes, I'll be sharing sections A and B with him, trying to keep my cool.

If he has something to say about the shit I pulled last night, he'll have a damn good chance of letting me know when he gets here.

I pull my bike into the parking lot of *Club Reckless* and hear the faint sound of music coming from the cornfield to the left of the building.

Smiling, I jump off my bike and head my ass down the beaten path to see Rowdy laying in the back of his truck surrounded by a cloud of smoke.

He's liked parking in the middle of the cornfield ever since I first met him at the age of sixteen. It's like his chill spot. So, I guess you can say him getting a job at the club was perfect for him.

The closer I get to his truck, I see him waving his arm around in the air while singing to Highly Suspect.

"It's just I'm not that good of a person," he sings at the top of his lungs, before taking a hit of his blunt and singing the next part. "But I might be enough for you. And I got enough love for two."

Rowdy's totally lost in his high and music, not even bothering to open his eyes until I'm jumping into the back of his truck to join him.

"Hey. Want some of this shit?" He taps my arm and holds out his blunt. "It's almost gone."

I shake my head. "Nah, man. It's all you."

He shrugs and takes two quick hits before putting it out with his fingers and shoving it into his shirt pocket.

"How long you been out here?" I reach into the cooler for a beer and pop the top off, hoping it will help me relax a bit before my shift starts.

"About an hour. It's so relaxing out here. No one fucks with you in the dark in the middle of a fucking cornfield." He laughs and reaches for his own beer now. "Cole stopped by my place earlier. He looked pretty tense and didn't say much. Just mentioned that Serge was filling in for him tonight."

Tilting my beer back, I take a moment to enjoy my drink before responding. I should've known Cole would need some time before seeing my ass after what I did to Brooke last night. "Yeah well. Let's just say I went to see his girl last night. My guess is he wants to kill me and is talking himself down from it."

Rowdy shakes his head and runs a hand through his messy hair, while releasing a deep breath. "You two are going to fuck things up for good if you keep going on like this. Then I'm stuck in the middle and shit."

I watch as he takes a swig of his beer, looking just about as stressed as I do now. He could be right.

"Maybe," I say. "But I can't stop until he knows what it felt like when he fucked me over. It hurt like a bitch and it still does. I can't sleep for shit without thinking about that night. It *fucking* haunts me, man. Besides . . . what I'm doing is far less shitty than what he did. He's been talking to this girl for what? A few weeks at most? I'm not doing anything but making him work harder to get her."

"I get it," he says, before taking a long drink of his beer and pulling out his stash of joints. "That's not something you'll easily get over and I wouldn't expect you too. Cole needs to pay for what he did. The fucker deserves it. But have you thought about what'll happen if you fall for his girl? Then what?"

I let out a small laugh. This dude must be *really* high, thinking all hard and shit. He seemed cool about this the other day. "That won't happen, Rowdy. She may be beautiful, but I'm going in this with my dick, not my heart. *This* is to get back at Cole and nothing more."

"Okay, motherfucker." He gives me a hard look, his bloodshot eyes wide. "And what about the girl? Does she get hurt in the process because of your guy's little fucking pissing match?"

"Fuck no," I growl out, my chest aching at the thought. Hurting her is the last thing I want to do. I'm not a heartless dick. "I'd never hurt Brooke. It's all about her pleasure and in the end, she can stay with Cole and everything will be good. I'll just be that guy she fucked and Cole will be the guy she fell for."

Rowdy doesn't look the least bit convinced. "And if she falls for both?"

"She won't. Fuck with the questions." I jump out of his truck and empty back the beer, before setting the empty bottle down. "I'll make sure of it."

"Hey!" Rowdy shouts as I walk away.

I stop and turn around. "What?"

"There's one thing you both should know." He smirks. "My

dick is bigger than the both of yours so if you both fall for her, I'll have to come in and steal her away."

"Alright, fucker." I shake my head and let out a small laugh. "I guess we'll see about that."

His music turns up and he goes back to singing, getting lost in his own little world again.

Let's hope it won't come down to that shit. No fucking falling . . .

I SHOULD'VE KNOWN WITH ALL the times I sent Katie away from my doorstep that she'd end up here at the club, hunting my ass down.

" . . . will you at least look at me?"

With my back pressed against the side of the building, I look up at her and blow out a steady stream of smoke. "The only reason I'm even out here right now with you is because you got Mason involved and he told me to get rid of your ass before you make a scene at his club."

I push away from the wall and get in her face, my muscles flexing when she reaches out and wraps her arms around my neck. "It hurts so much. Jameson–"

"No," I growl, cutting her off. "You should've thought about how much it'd hurt when you were riding my best friend's dick. I hope it felt really fucking good as he filled you. Because if it didn't . . ." I lean in to speak against her lips. "You lost me for nothing."

I can't stand to even look at her.

Turning away from her, I snatch her hands away from me and begin walking around to the front of the building, making it clear this conversation is over before she can get it started. "Stop being a fucking stalker and move on."

"No," she yells out, grabbing my arm to try and force me to stop walking. "Fucking stop being this way. I want to be with you."

She slaps my arm when I continue to walk away from her, as if she's just a bother.

"You're an asshole! Don't walk away from me."

I laugh. "I'm the nicest asshole you could ever hope to meet. Trust me, babe. Now. Leave. Me. Alone."

Getting angry, she rushes around to slap my chest, before pushing me.

I stand here, just taking it, letting her get it all out, in hopes she'll fuck off after this.

Her hits get harder with each swing, causing me to flex my chest and abs.

"What the fuck is going on over here?" We both look over at the sound of Brooke's voice. "Being a woman doesn't give you the right to hit a man."

Seeing her sends my heart into overdrive, pounding with excitement as I look her over in her ripped up jeans and high heeled boots.

I didn't expect her to be here tonight since Cole took the night off. It's a nice surprise.

"This is a private conversation," Katie chokes out, while stepping away from me. "It doesn't concern you so leave us alone."

Brooke seems to be amused by Katie's words, keeping her eyes on her as she walks over and wraps her arms around my waist as if to get me away from her.

Her voice is tight as she speaks. "Are you fucking joking? You're putting your hands all over Jameson after he clearly asked you to leave him alone. He may be man enough to stand there and take it, but I'm a woman and I won't just stand back and watch."

Katie's eyes widen as she steps back and looks Brooke over, most likely sizing her up to see if she can take her. She looks both jealous and scared by the time she's done scanning her out.

"You sure were quick to find someone to sink your dick into. Congratulations on pushing me away for good." She yanks off the necklace I bought her for her birthday last year and tosses it at me. "You really are an asshole and I hate you. I tried. I fucking tried and this is what I get. After four years. Goodbye, Jameson. You better hope she can handle you sexually like I did. Not many women can, asshole. She'll become boring after a week."

With that, she stomps off across the parking lot, pushing some innocent girl out of her way to get over to her car.

Brooke releases my waist and takes a step away, putting space between us once we're alone. "I hate women like that. Sorry to butt in, but I figured you could use my help to get rid of her."

I smile down at her, causing her to smile back. "What? Sometimes men need a little help too."

I shake my head and pull out a cigarette, getting comfortable against the building. "I've never met someone before that could shut Katie up. I'm just thankful and *very* impressed."

She laughs and leans against the building beside me. "I've dealt with a lot of intolerable people in the years I've been in the bar business. I guess you can say I don't take bullshit very well."

"Good to hear." I take a drag of my cigarette and close my eyes as I slowly exhale. "I'm the same way. That's why my ex won't leave me alone."

"I kind of gathered she was an ex," Brooke says on a laugh. "They're the hardest to get rid of and she didn't seem to want to give you up." Her eyes look me over, before she pulls them away and gently says, "I don't blame her."

Taking one last drag, I toss my cigarette down and place my hands against the building, pinning her in with my arms.

"Is that right?"

She nods and meets my eyes.

"Why is that?" I push.

A small rush of air escapes her as I spread her thighs with my leg and press my body between them.

"Because you've barely even touched me, yet my body craves more of you. I can't imagine how she must feel after experiencing all you have to offer."

I feel my dick growing hard against her body as I listen to her words.

"Like right now . . ." she breathes. "I'm going crazy inside having you this close to me."

"I'd be happy to give you *everything* I gave her, Brooke. I just need to know one thing . . ."

She steps up on the tip of her toes to whisper in my ear, her breath sending chills down my body. I love her being bold with me. "What's that?"

"That you can handle having us both and only falling for Cole."

She doesn't say anything for a few seconds as if she's thinking it over in her head.

"I figured that's what you and Cole had in mind after that little show you gave me in my apartment. That is why Cole fucked me harder than he ever has before, right? It turns you both on to see who can work me up the most?" She wraps her arm around my neck and gently bites my ear. "For the record . . . I've never been more turned on in my life. Doesn't mean I'm ready to fall for anyone and if I do, I'll make sure it's Cole. I'm tough. I can handle more than you think."

Just as I'm about to speak, we get interrupted by her friend, coming around the corner, calling out for her.

"Brooke! You back there creeping in the dark like some psycho?"

Brooke clears her throat and releases her hold on my neck, laughing into my chest, before speaking. "Yeah, back here."

"Oh good." Karson smiles and looks us over once she reaches us. "Didn't mean to interrupt any wild sex that might've been close to taking place, but we gotta get going."

The thought of Brooke leaving has me pushing away from the building and running my hand through my hair. I'm feeling extremely sexually frustrated and I'm not ready to let her out of my sight yet. "You're not staying?"

"Can't," she replies, looking just as sexually frustrated as I am. "Just stopped in to say hi. Karson wanted to get your friend's number really quick and he told me where to find you." She steps away from the building and joins her friend. "I have a job interview at some karaoke bar about five minutes from here. Real fun stuff."

Our eyes stay locked as she begins backing up. "Goodbye, Jameson."

I smile to myself as she turns the other way and continues walking. "Good luck, babe."

She smiles over her shoulder, but doesn't say anything as her and Karson disappear back around the building.

Not even two seconds later, Serge speaks into the earpiece calling me back inside.

So much for hiding this massive fucking boner Brooke left me with.

Looks like she has a feisty side, just waiting to come out and play with us . . .

CHAPTER TEN

Brooke

K ARSON'S EYES MIGHT JUST POP out of the sockets if she doesn't stop staring at me so damn hard right now.

I mean . . . I suppose it *is* my fault. I guess I kind of forgot to mention the hot little fact that I watched Jameson pleasure himself in my apartment last night.

Not that I haven't been thinking about it, because trust me; I have. *A lot. A whole lot.*

I was barely able to keep my cool when I saw him just a few minutes ago, outside of the club. My whole body ached, screaming out to touch him in the dirtiest way possible.

Especially after seeing him standing there, all manly and sexy, while his ex was pushing and hitting at his firm chest.

Not saying it didn't piss me off she touched him, because trust me, I wanted to knock her out for laying her bitchy little hands on him like that.

But something about the way he closed his eyes and took it,

made me think he's got a lot of respect for women. Most other guys would've knocked her on her ass by then.

He was just going to stand there and accept the blows, until I came along.

"Say what?" Karson throws her seatbelt off and laughs, unsure of what to think of my words. "Wait . . . you're serious?"

The heated look on my face must give away my answer, because she instantly stops laughing, straightening up in her seat. "Oh my God! I thought you were joking. He came to your apartment last night and what? Just whipped it out and stroked it for you?"

I feel an ache between my legs, remembering in my head how it all went down. It was by far one of the sexiest things a man has ever done for me.

"Well . . . not exactly." I undo my seatbelt and reach up to fix my sloppy bun. "It was a whole lot sexier than just that. It's hard to explain."

She laughs. "I bet it is *hard* . . . and big. Was it big?"

I let out a slow breath and lean my head into the headrest, now picturing its size and how big it looked, even in his strong hands. "Yes," I breathe. "You have no idea."

Grinning, she pulls her keys out of the ignition, keeping her eyes on me. "Bigger than Cole's?"

I smile, but stay silent, not wanting to get into this talk right now. Knowing Karson, she'll want me to describe the differences in detail.

Honestly, they're close in size, but I think Jameson might just have an inch on Cole. That's something I couldn't help but to notice, the second it sprang free from his pants.

"Let's go," I say, instead, while opening the door. "We don't have time for the details I know your dirty little mind is dying to get. I'm late."

This earns a growl out of Karson along with a few very colorful words, but she quickly follows me through the parking lot.

The horrible sound of screeching or singing—I'm not quite sure yet—fills my ears when we enter *BJ's Place*, stopping in the doorway.

It's a lot more crowded in the bar than I expected and it surprises me. It might possibly be worth my time after all.

"Woah!" Karson screams next to my ear all giddy like, while looking around at all the pretty lights. "This place looks pretty damn fun. I likie a lot."

Checking the place out, I begin walking, with Karson following closely behind. She seems to be a little more amused than I am by this place, but I think I'm liking it.

There's two girls dancing around the small stage in the center of the room, singing loudly into mics, not giving two shits what they sound like.

Seems like the perfect place for Karson to be vocal.

"Yeah, I could see you working here. Maybe you should quit that boring diner job you're always bitching about and apply here with me."

I can just imagine a big, cheesy smile taking over her face right about now, giving some serious thought into what I just suggested.

"Will you do karaoke with me if I do?" She speeds up to jump in front of me, cutting me off right before I can grab for a barstool and get the bartender's attention. "Give me that and I'll join you right here in sweet karaoke hell."

I laugh and look over, watching as the room begins to join in at the end of the song, everyone going crazy.

It has excitement coursing through me, making me want to join in and have fun too. That's exactly what I was missing at *Diamond's*.

"Sure. Why the hell not?"

Grinning like a maniac, Karson grabs my arms and begins

dancing next to me, belting out the last few lyrics to *Cool for the Summer* by Demi Lovato.

"I fucking love you!" she screams in my face. "Let's find this Ben person and get my ass an application. Ben!"

I can't help but to smile as she begins cupping her hands over her face like a megaphone as she screams his name a few more times.

As crazy as she looks right now, it gets the attention of the bartender who nods to us, before walking into the back to most likely grab poor Ben.

He seriously has no idea what he's getting into if he gives us both a job here, working at the same time.

"That's one way to get noticed. Nice job, babe."

She gives me a satisfied look and pulls out the stool next to me, hopping onto it. "You're welcome. In a place like this, the loudest ones always stand out."

"He'll be out in a minute. Here . . ." The female bartender slides two shots our way and slaps the bar. "Good luck."

With that, she looks away from us and begins waving her arms around, dancing as the next song begins to play.

She looks to be enjoying herself, which definitely has me more excited about the possibility of this job now.

Karson and I both bring our attention to some guy when he shoves his head in between us and starts singing to the current song.

He's cute, which has us both spinning around to watch him as he begins dancing and motioning for us to follow him.

"That's Ben!" the bartender points out to us. "He's crazy but harmless. Go."

I can't help the smile that takes over as we follow him through the bar and to some room down the hall.

"Welcome, ladies," he says with a friendly smile, while holding open a door for us. "Let's get you inside my office where it's quieter."

He offers us a seat and then takes one himself at the edge of his beaten-up desk, while running a hand through his blonde hair and smiling at us. "One of you lovely ladies must be Brooke. Which one?"

I offer him a smile when his eyes land on me. "I'm Brooke and the loud, crazy chick next to me that was screaming your name is Karson. Just to warn you, she's looking for a job too."

"I am," she jumps in. "I can't promise I'll stay away from the mic while I'm working so I want to throw that out there, too."

Ben laughs as if he's not the least bit surprised. "I wouldn't expect you to, but thanks for the honesty. Here . . ." He reaches behind him for an application and hands it to Karson. "Fill this out and we'll give you both a chance. Let's say . . . tomorrow night around six. Just bring the application back then."

"Sounds fantastic to me. Looking forward to it."

Nodding, he jumps off the desk and walks around to take a seat behind it. "Perfect. Now get the hell out of my office and have some fun. Tell Ariel drinks are on me tonight."

Surprised, we both thank Ben and leave his office, anxious to just let loose for a bit and enjoy some girl time.

Two drinks and three shots later, we find ourselves on stage singing our asses off to *Like a Prayer* by Madonna.

Half the bar joins in with us, a lot of women joining us on stage dancing as if no one's watching.

We sing and dance so hard for the next few hours that, my throat begins hurting and I find myself fighting to catch my breath and cool off, while stripping off my outer tank top and tossing it aside.

"Karson," I yell over at her. "I'll be back."

I've had to use the bathroom for at least an hour now, but we've been having way too much fun, so I've been putting it off until now.

I *really* need to go. And we all know once you break that stupid magical seal, you'll be in the bathroom every ten minutes.

She stops singing to yell at me. "What?"

I point toward the bathroom door and begin backing up. "Bathroom."

She gives me a thumbs up and goes back to looking for her next song to slaughter. She'll most likely make me join her on that one as well. "Hurry back. We're next."

Laughing, I spin around on my heels, my whole body seeming to freeze, my heart jumping into overdrive, the moment my eyes land on a certain someone sitting at the bar.

Jameson . . .

He looks soooo damn sexy as he flashes me a smile from above his glass, before tilting it back and emptying what's left of it.

I definitely wasn't expecting to see him again tonight. Holy fuck . . .

CHAPTER ELEVEN

Jameson

S OMEWHERE BETWEEN THE CLUB AND my house, I
made the decision to take a little detour to check out this
karaoke bar Brooke mentioned she was getting a job at.

I never expected her to still be here when I arrived. But when I
saw her friend's car out in the parking lot, I couldn't resist stopping
in for a drink.

So, I've been sitting here, throwing back a glass of whiskey
for the last twenty minutes, watching Brooke cut loose and sing
with her friend.

It's kept me smiling since I sat down. To be honest, it's probably
one of the best times I've had in a while, without thinking about
all the bullshit that's been bringing me down.

What has me smiling even more is the fact she's just *now*
noticed me here.

From the look on her face as she stands there frozen, watching
me, I'd say she's both shocked and excited to see me.

I've always loved that combination on a woman.

She's staring awfully hard, her eyes burning into me, as I tilt my glass back, finishing my drink off. The one drink I allowed myself to have so I'd be sober enough to do this next part.

Setting my empty glass down, I toss a tip on the bar, being sure to watch Brooke's reaction to me as I stand.

The closer I get to her, the more anxious her eyes seem to become as she looks me over, being sure to take in every inch of me.

"What are you doing here?" she asks, once I stop in front of her. "I mean . . ." she laughs and brushes her sweaty hair from her face. "I didn't mean for it to sound that way. I just didn't expect you to be here."

"That makes two of us." She sucks in a small breath, when I reach out and brush the stray piece of hair out of her face she seemed to miss. "Come with me."

Her eyes widen as if she's surprised by my request, but I can see the curiosity beginning to come out as she speaks. "Right now? The bars are about to close though."

I nod my head. "Doesn't matter. We're not going to another bar."

"What about Karson? I came here with her."

I look over Brooke's shoulder to see Karson dancing around the stage with two girls. She seems to be having fun just fine without Brooke.

"Tell her you're getting a ride with me and to look outside for Rowdy when the bar closes down." I nod toward the stage, where she's still dancing around with a mic. "She'll be fine with her new friends for a bit."

Brooke seems to think this over for a few seconds, before she turns back to look at me with an amused laugh. "I think you're right. She's to that point now where anyone and everyone is her best friend. I'm sure she won't mind. Besides, it'll rescue me from having to sing a hundredth song for the night."

Without saying another word, she walks over to the stage and grabs Karson's arm to get her attention.

This has her friend looking over at me, giving me a thumbs up, as Brooke speaks into her ear.

I offer her a smile, feeling my heart race as Brooke walks back over to me and wraps her arm around my neck, pulling me in so she can talk. "I'll meet you outside. Just have to use the bathroom before we leave."

"I'll be right outside the door."

I just hope she likes fast bikes.

I have a feeling we can both use a little adrenaline rush tonight and I plan to give her just that.

As she walks away, I send a quick text to Rowdy, before shoving my phone in my pocket and heading for the door.

I don't even make it two feet, when some brunette grabs onto me from out of nowhere and pulls me down close to her. "Come sing with me?"

"Sorry, babe." I offer her a smile and remove her hands from my chest. "I'm just leaving with someone."

"Such a shame." She shakes her head and gives me a pouty face. "I've had my eye on you since you walked through that door. Guess I should've made my move sooner."

She backs away from me, looking my body up and down, before spinning on her heels and rushing over to a group of her friends.

They all seem to look my way, while she most likely tells them everything we just said.

Now, that I'm free again, I make my way outside and across the parking lot to where my Hayabusa is parked.

Straddling it, I place my helmet in my lap and look up to see Brooke exiting the bar, right as I start the engine.

A confident smile takes over as I sit here for a moment and watch her looking around her as if she's worried I've left without her.

Nah, I just had to park all the way across the lot since this place is packed tonight. There's no way I'd leave here without her.

I'm ready for a little fun tonight. Hell, it's been a long damn time since I've played on my bike and I want her to see just how in control I'm in.

Gripping my bike, I take off slowly and lean forward until my weight is over the handlebars. Once I'm in front of Brooke with her facing my direction, I squeeze the front brake, making the back wheel come off the pavement.

She watches me in wonder as my front wheel comes to a stop *right* in front of her legs, before my back wheel comes back down to meet the ground.

Her body is more than safe and well looked after in my hands. I'm known for being a little reckless, but I'm even more well known for taking care of a woman's body.

Brooke's eyes widen as if she's impressed with my little stunt, but I can see behind her wonder that she's a little nervous about getting on this thing. "That was pretty amazing. How did . . ." She shakes her head and smiles as if she doesn't know what to say. "I've never been on a motorcycle before, Jameson. I'm a little nervous, although I have a feeling you're pretty in control."

I grab her hand and pull her to me, before sliding my helmet on her head with a smirk. "I'm well in control. You're safe in my hands. Just hold on tight."

Without any hesitation, she hops on the back of my bike and wraps her arms around my waist, holding on for dear life. "I'm ready." She yells over my shoulder. "Holy shit," I hear her say against my back. "I can't believe I'm doing this."

Filled with adrenaline, I take off, turning down a side road for now, that I know will have less traffic.

I want her to get comfortable with being on my bike, before I have fun with her. She needs to know she's good with me, so I don't scare her away from ever getting back on my bike.

So, we ride through the light traffic for about twenty minutes, her remaining calm as I weave my way through traffic, being sure to keep us safe.

I just want to give her a taste of what it feels like to let loose on this damn thing and feel free for a while.

"I trust you," she says, while moving her hands up higher to wrap around my chest. "You can go fast now. I'm ready."

I smile and reach my hand back to scoot her ass closer to me. "Stay against me. Tap me if you need me to slow down."

Pulling out onto the open road, I lean forward, and take off fast, feeling her body mold to mine as she buries her face into my back.

No other vehicles are around, giving us the space to own the road and reach ninety mph.

My bike can reach up to one-eighty-six, but there's no way in hell I'd do that with her on the back of it.

Knowing she's trusting me with her life right now, gives me a rush. Katie never trusted my bike. Even though she's seen me do many tricks on it in the past.

"Faster, Jameson," Brooke yells over my shoulder, while squeezing me.

Smiling, I speed up until we reach one-ten, giving her the rush she's asking for. She's squeezing me so damn tightly I can barely breathe. Her nails are now digging into my chest, making me want to stop this bike so I can fuck her.

It turns me on when a woman is rough with my body.

So, I gradually slow us back down to sixty, to get her grip on me to loosen up.

I feel my breathing pick up as her hands lower down my body, her fingertips taking their time over every ridge of muscle as if she's turned on by being on the back of my bike.

Well, I'm definitely turned on with having her on the back.

"Fuck," I growl to myself, before pulling over and helping her off the back. I can't handle her hands on me right now. I'm going to end up doing something really fucking stupid and outside of my plan if she continues.

Turning off my bike, I jump off and step over to her, grabbing for my helmet, before tossing it down into the grass.

My chest moves fast, as I flex my jaw and take my time, looking over her beautiful fucking body.

I'm fighting with everything in me right now, not to just set her on the back of my bike and fuck her.

I want to hear her scream and feel her nails dig into my flesh as I pound into her, taking her deep. So *fucking* deep.

"Something wrong?" Brooke questions, her confused eyes meeting mine as she breathes heavily, still trying to come down from our rush. "Something upset you?"

Without saying a word, I throw my leg over my bike, straddling it backwards, before I grab her hips and pull her close. "Not at all. I just wanted to stop and do this for a moment."

Gripping her hips, I lean back and pull her against my bike, letting her know I want her to straddle my lap.

I can see the pulse in her neck quicken as she holds onto my arm and climbs on top of me.

Keeping my feet planted on the ground for support, I grab the back of her neck and pull it toward me so I can speak into her ear. "It would be so hot to fuck you right here on the back of my bike. You have no idea how much restraint it's taking not too." I push her body down, grinding my hard cock between her legs. "Ever rode someone's dick on the back of a fast bike?"

She shakes her head and releases a breath as my thumb brushes over the front of her neck, before my hand wraps around it. "I would let you ride my dick right now to show you what it feels like, but Cole doesn't know I'm with you."

I can feel her body shake above mine, as she most likely imagines what it would be like if I fucked her here on my bike.

It has me grinding my cock harder between her legs.

"Yeah," she breathes, while placing her hand on my chest and digging her fingers in. "So, that's the difference from the night you showed up at my apartment. He knew you'd be there giving me a show. Is that your guy's thing?"

"Yes," I admit, with my jaw clenched tightly. "Let's just say it makes the other person work harder at pleasuring you. But I'm not meant to fuck you alone, Brooke. I might cross that line if I don't get you back soon. My plans tonight, weren't supposed to involve stopping by the karaoke bar."

Her nails dig into my arm as I grind my hips into her again and squeeze her neck tighter. "I can't handle this, Jameson. I just." Her voice begins to shake with pleasure. "I can't help myself when it comes to you. It's like my whole fucking body just aches to feel you. It's stupid . . . I know. This never happens to me."

My cock hardens even more from her words as I watch her lips move so damn close to mine, just waiting to be tasted. They're so fucking sexy that I want nothing more than to say fuck it and kiss her. "I probably shouldn't do this. But fuck it."

With a growl, I crush my lips against hers, tugging and pulling as I slide a hand down between our bodies, shoving it into the front of her jeans.

I need to feel her right now. It took every bit of my restraint not to, that night at her apartment, but she's too damn close for me not to.

Brooke leans her head back and moans out as I slide my finger over her wetness, before shoving it into her pussy and roughly biting her neck.

I can feel her heart hammering against my chest as I begin to slide my finger in and out, before shoving a second finger inside and stopping.

This pussy is sure to send me over the edge soon.

"Why do you have to be so wet for me?" I question against her ear, angry with my damn self. "It has me stingy as fuck, making me want to *fuck* you right here and right now. I've always wanted to take someone on my bike. I always tend to fuck on ones that aren't *mine.*"

Her hands move around my body to grab onto my back, her nails digging into my shirt as I begin to move my hips into her as if we're fucking. "Then do it, Jameson?" she breathes in desperation. "I've been wanting you to since you bought me that shot. And you knew the second you walked into my apartment you'd have me wanting you even more by the time you left. You *did* this to me."

She's right, there. I wanted to get under her skin and make her want me. It worked.

"I fucking can't." I pump my fingers into her pussy a few more times, knowing she's so damn close to coming undone in my lap. "But you can imagine my dick going in and out of you, instead of my fingers."

Her moans become louder and she begins grinding her hips above me, getting desperate for release now. "That's it." I squeeze a third finger inside, because she's going to need a lot more than just a couple of fingers to imagine it's my dick she's riding.

I'd use a forth if I thought it'd fit, but fuck, she's so damn tight.

It would be so easy to just say fuck Cole and take her right here, but that's not what I had in mind when I decided I was going to make him work for Brooke.

My plan was to make her want me enough to the point she'd beg Cole to let her have us both at the same time.

Not to fuck her behind Cole's back and build any kind of attachment. Even if I do hate him for what he did to me. That's the last thing I want. She still needs to fall for Cole.

I need to be careful with Brooke or I could screw this whole thing up.

"I want to touch you when I come for you," she says quickly, out of breath. "Let me touch you."

One look into her demanding eyes and I know I'm going to give her what she wants.

Even with the car coming down the road, toward us, I reach down with my free hand and undo my pants, pulling my hard cock out.

Satisfied, Brooke reaches for it, taking it in both hands as I continue to finger fuck her.

"Holy shit . . ." she breathes. "Keep going. Keep going . . ."

I find myself beginning to moan out as she strokes me, her hands running over my dick as if she owns it.

It has me losing control, so I pull my hand out of her jeans, and pick her up, setting her down on my bike so I can get off.

Breathing heavily, she digs her heels into the dirt, looking up at me, confused.

"Turn around," I demand.

Doing as told, she spins around so she's facing the back of my bike, just like I was.

This allows me to rip her jeans open and yank them down her legs, so she's left in her red thong and high heeled boots.

I take a second to enjoy the view of her of straddling my bike half-naked, while I stroke myself for her like I did the other night.

She watches me, with a need that's driving her mad. I'd say I more than did my part of making her want me.

I just didn't expect to want her just as much or even more. I'm fighting so damn hard not to just slide her panties to the side and slip inside of her, owning her pussy.

"Fuck . . . come here." I grab the back of her neck and guide her closer to me.

Her eyes lower to my chest as I pull my t-shirt off and throw it in the grass, giving her a nice view to get off to, since I've already covered my cock back up.

I had to or I knew it'd get me into bigger trouble than I'm looking for.

Pushing her panties to the side, I slide my fingers back in, pumping in and out as I lean in to kiss her.

The way her tongue flicks out to lick my bottom lip as I pull away is almost enough to make me kiss her again, but I know the kissing needs to fucking stop.

Her taste has me craving to suck and devour her lips as if they're mine to own, but they're not. Kissing her feels too damn good for me to continue it without losing control.

Fuuuuck!

I need to finish getting her off so I can get her home, before I end up doing the biggest asshole thing I can do.

A few pumps later and I feel her clench around my fingers as she bites my shoulder.

"Oh shit, Jameson . . ." Her breath is heavy against my skin as she comes down from her orgasm. "This . . . this was one of the hottest, craziest things I've ever done." She looks toward the road as another car passes us. That's when I feel her laugh against my chest, realizing anyone could've seen us if they stopped long enough to look.

"You weren't worried about someone seeing us?" I grin as her hands run down my bare chest and abs, before she reaches into my pants and begins stroking my cock.

"No." She bites her bottom lip and continues to stroke me as if I'm hers, to do what she pleases with. "It only made it more exciting. I like not knowing what to expect."

"Fuck, Brooke . . ." I lean my head back and close my eyes, enjoying her hands all over my body.

Each place she touches me feels as if it's on fire, from her the feel of her skin.

It's a reminder of what I need to do.

"Fucking shit . . ." I growl, while stopping her hands from touching me. "I can't handle your hands on me without wanting to lose control and when I lose control, there's no fucking stopping it."

Turning away from me, she lets out a frustrated breath and leans back on the seat. "You and Cole need to stop this torturing and take me already. It's too much to take."

"You want us to fuck you at the same time?"

My question has her sitting up to look at me. "It's all I've been able to think about for days. I've never been so sexually frustrated in my life."

I grab her hand and help her off my bike, us both quickly getting decent again.

"Then, I'll make sure that happens. You just better make sure you can handle the both of us. It's not just some fifteen minute thing. It's an all night deal when it comes to us."

She looks a little nervous, but nods her head and grabs the back of my neck, pulling my face down so our lips are almost touching. "I can handle it. Don't worry about me."

Smiling with satisfaction, I reach for my helmet and slide it back on Brooke's head, before helping her on my bike.

Looks like it's time to get my buddy Cole on board . . .

CHAPTER TWELVE

Jameson

O N THE RIDE TO MY house, thoughts of Brooke's soft lips against mine fucking consume me, making it hard to think clearly.

It wasn't supposed to feel as good as it did. I wasn't supposed to want to keep kissing her and claim her as my own, but I did.

That's exactly why I had to put a stop to things tonight, before it was too late. Apparently, being alone with Brooke is a bad idea. Something I'm now very aware of.

I need to be careful when it comes to her. One wrong touch could be enough to change the game. One wrong kiss could be enough to destroy it.

My intentions were to get under her skin just enough to make her want me sexually. I wanted Cole to feel what it's like, knowing someone he's supposed to trust has been inside his girl.

All I wanted was something strong enough to make me forget how he betrayed me. Something a lot fucking stronger than the bottom of a damn whiskey bottle, because all that seems to do is temporally numb the pain.

That's not good enough for me anymore.

I need it to go away completely and the only thing my fucked-up mind can come up with is to make him feel my pain.

Damn, I'm an asshole.

When I dropped Brooke off at home, I half expected Cole to be waiting outside for her, ready to rip my head off.

Taking her alone, to the middle of nowhere, was probably a shitty thing on my part. Ruining his chance with Brooke isn't what I'm going for, yet I came so damn close to just giving in and fucking her.

It took every bit of restraint not to. Especially knowing how badly she wanted me to.

"Well, what do you know."

My whole body tenses up when I pull up in front of my house to see Cole's Charger parked in the driveway.

The car's not running and I don't see him leaning against it, so I can only assume he somehow got one of Rowdy's keys to let himself inside.

Leave it up to Rowdy's high ass to keep a stockpile of my keys since he keeps losing and finding them. Last I checked his ass had at least ten "safely" tucked away in a drawer.

Safe my ass . . .

Feeling tense, I take in a deep breath and slowly release it as I slide my helmet off and walk into my already open front door.

My eyes immediately land on Cole relaxing with a drink in hand, in the chair that sits in front of the fireplace.

"I hope there's enough whiskey left for two," I say stiffly. "I have a feeling we're going to need it."

He smirks and holds up an unopened bottle. "Don't I always come prepared?"

I toss my helmet and keys down, keeping my eyes on him as he reaches beside him to fill a second glass.

"That's the only reason we've been friends for twenty years."

He hands me a glass with a sideways smile. "I can't argue that shit. Whiskey can help even the most fucked up friendships stay intact."

I grab the drink from his hand and take a huge chug, closing my eyes as the burn fills my throat. "Ah, fuck. I love that feeling."

The room's quiet for a few moments as I take a seat in the chair across from Cole's.

Sometimes you just need a few moments of silence while enjoying a glass of regret with your asshole friends.

"I went to go see Brooke," he says. "Was hoping she'd miss my handsome ass, but then realized she must've been with my *almost* as equally handsome friend so . . ."

"I didn't fuck her," I growl. "I'm not that low. I may hate your piece of shit ass right now, but I'm not trying to *take* Brooke from you."

He shakes his head, while pouring himself a second glass. "I get it. I know you're pissed at me for what I did to you and this is your way of getting back at me. It's how we fucking function because we're two screwed up assholes."

"I won't argue that." I finish my drink off before slamming it down on the table. "Why are you here, Cole? You here to fight or just sit in front of a fire and snuggle with the one person you hate right now? I can grab the fucking marshmallows and we can make a night of it."

My words cause him to laugh and stand up to refill my glass. "I'm here because I want this shit to be over with. I want a chance to explain why I did what I did that night so we can both move on from this crap."

"What makes you think anything you say is going to be good

enough to make me just forgive you as if it never fucking happened?"

He sits up straight and flexes his jaw. "I don't expect that shit to happen. But I do expect you to stop hating me at some point and open your eyes to the piece of shit Katie was."

I feel my blood boil from his words. He always did try to tell me she wasn't good enough for me. That all she was doing was bringing me down.

So why not just fuck her to get her out of my life, right? I wasn't willing to get rid of her so he did.

"Fucking Katie, wasn't doing me any favors, asshole. It was doing yourself a favor."

"The fuck it was." He looks extremely agitated and stressed as he begins pacing in front of my chair. "You were too blind to see how she was dragging you down. She had you stressed the fuck out to the point you began to think it was just every day normal life. I couldn't even remember a time when you didn't drink yourself to sleep every damn night. That's when I knew it was time to step in and save your ass. 'Cause you sure in the hell wasn't going to do it."

I feel my chest tighten as I let his words sink in. Katie was the love of my life. At least, that's what I'd been telling myself since the day she walked up and kissed me.

She consumed me. Made it hard to think about anything other than her. She made sure of that by keeping me sexually pleased, allowing me to take her as rough and wild as I wanted. I was in control when it came to our sex life, but maybe that was her way of controlling me outside of it.

"She accused you almost every other day of cheating on her. You know who does that? Cheaters. That's who. Her guilty conscience of sleeping around on you had her worried you were doing the same."

I sit, in silence, the guilt beginning to creep in as his words unravel her hold on me, making it clear what she'd been doing to me over the years.

At one point, I assumed she was cheating on me. Hell, I even had someone tell me she was, but I refused to believe it.

Our healthy sex life kept me blind to that possibility and she always managed to talk her way around it and come up with alibis.

"All I wanted was to have my best friend back. You're my brother, Jameson. Her bringing you down was bringing me down. It fucking hurt to see you hurt. So yeah, I took extreme measures, knowing damn well you'd probably hate me. So, fuck you, but I did it for you."

His words have my head spinning and me beginning to lose my shit. Now, I'm the one pacing like a maniac.

"Fuuuck!"

Reaching for the closest thing to me, I throw it across the room, the glass breaking against the fireplace.

All my rage for Cole is turning to guilt.

Guilt for wanting to hurt him. Guilt for making him work for his girl. Fuck, guilt for wanting his girl.

"I'm sorry, man." I stand with my hands in my hair, trying to think of how to make this better. "I don't know what the fuck was wrong with me. When I heard about you and Katie, it had my head all screwed up."

"Love. That's what was wrong with you. I don't blame you for that. Katie was a fucking she-devil bitch. She was good."

I find myself laughing and reaching for my whiskey. "At least Brooke is different."

"She's a good one," he says from behind me. "And as much as we both screwed up, I think she deserves to get what she wants now."

I stop mid-drink to turn around and look at him. "Me messing with her was a dickhead move on my part. I'll leave her alone now."

"It's too late, man." He grabs my drink from my hand and finishes it off. "The only way to get you out of her system is for her to experience with you. She's a good woman. This isn't about you or me anymore. It's about her and we're going to give her what she desires."

I just keep staring at him like a fucking idiot, because I have no clue what to say right now.

After all this shit, he still wants me to share his girl with him.

"It's not like we haven't shared before. It worked out in the past and it'll work out now." He grips my shoulder and smirks. "Besides, once she has us both she'll clearly realize how much better I am."

"You're a delusional asshole."

"Keep telling yourself that." He sets down my empty glass and reaches for his jacket. "I heard you're having a party this weekend. Let's show Brooke a good time."

"You sure about this shit?"

"For her . . . yeah. Besides if she wants to experience a three-some, we're the best two out there. I mean . . . look at us."

"Again, I can't argue there."

With that he takes off, leaving me to stand in front of the fire-place, thinking of how the hell I'm going to pull this off without getting any feelings involved.

After my kiss with Brooke earlier, this is going to be harder than I thought. And now that Cole and I are friends again, falling for his girl is the last thing I can allow myself to do . . .

CHAPTER THIRTEEN

Brooke

MY HEART PRACTICALLY BEATS OUT of my chest as I stare through the windshield at the big white house in front of me. I can't believe I'm sitting outside Jameson's place, about to attend a party that *Cole* invited me to.

Not even three days ago, I was on the back of Jameson's motorcycle receiving one of the best orgasms of my life, practically on the verge of begging him to take me. And now, here I am, meeting his friend at *his* party.

This is far from normal, but I have a feeling things with the boys are anything but.

They've done this kind of thing before. I'm not the first woman they've teamed up on and to be honest, I feel insanely lucky I'm getting the chance to experience them.

Even if things are bound to become messy, this . . . this feels so fucking fantastic, both mentally and physically.

When I received the text from Cole two hours ago, inviting

me to join him at Jameson's party, my first reaction was to rush home from work and take a quick shower so I could look my best for them both.

I can't even begin to explain the adrenaline that was running through me when I responded back with a yes.

It was as if my fingers couldn't type fast enough.

I need these boys. I want them, desperately.

As long as I have control over my feelings, then I see no reason why being here with Cole will end up as a disaster.

Surely, both men know I've been invited and both men know by *whom*.

I close my eyes and press my fingers to my lips as I remember the way Jameson kissed me on the side of the road the other night.

This is not what I should be thinking about right now.

Yes, his kiss felt good. In fact, it felt more than good. It felt fucking magical.

It was as if my entire body ignited, heat taking over every inch of me, until it felt as if my skin was on fire.

It completely shocked me, but I was so lost in the moment I couldn't think rationally enough to make myself stop and question the feeling.

All I know is I wanted more of whatever it was that was taking over me.

Don't get me wrong, Cole's kiss is damn good too, but something about the way Jameson moved against me with such demand and control had my heart and body reacting.

His kiss alone was enough to set me off and make me forget about everything around me.

Cole had no idea I was with Jameson, yet, worrying about how that might make him feel was the last thing on my mind.

It was as if I trusted Jameson to do what he knew was best for me. I let him have control and it felt nice for once.

Giving up control isn't something I allow myself to do often.

Except of course, when it comes to both Cole and Jameson. Making sure not to give up too much control is going to be the hard part.

Giving up too much control means falling and falling for both is the last thing I can do.

Hell, I'm not even sure allowing myself to fall for even one is a good idea.

It could complicate their friendship, which is another clue for me that Cole is looking to keep things between us casual. Just as I suspected in the beginning.

Otherwise . . . why share with his friend? Why risk losing their friendship if things happen to become complicated?

I don't know what I'd do if me and Karson ever broke up our friendship due to falling for the same damn guy. I'd probably never get past it.

It would destroy me.

Fun. That's all this is. For all of us.

Karson must notice my internal conflict, because it's easy to catch her staring at me from my peripheral vision. She's looking hard, as if I've been lost in my head for way too long and I probably have by now.

"Honey . . . you okay over there? You look like you're having a mental breakdown? Is there something I don't know? Should we skip the party?"

I release a quick breath and eagerly shake my head, not wanting her to worry about me. If I let on to the fact that something is bothering me, then we'll spend the next hour in this vehicle while she questions me.

I'm a grown ass woman. I can figure this out and keep a straight head.

I have to. I'm going in there with confidence and owning this moment. After the shitty men I've had; I deserve this night.

"I'm good. I'm ready." I throw my seatbelt off and turn to face her with a smile. "You ready?"

She smiles back and reaches for her purse. "I've been ready since the second I heard Rowdy would be gracing this party with his hotness. I haven't seen him since he gave me a ride home the night you took off with Jameson."

I swallow and pretend as if mention of that night isn't reminding me of the intensity of Jameson's kiss again.

Tonight—none of that needs to matter.

"Alrighty . . . let's go, then."

I feel curiosity and excitement take over when I look over to see Cole's car parked right behind Jameson's motorcycle.

The two men that have been driving me crazy with this need I've never felt before, will be here, in the same house, hopefully giving me what my body so desperately needs.

Them.

Without even knocking, Karson pushes the door open, letting herself inside. A smile takes over as she whiffs the air. "Smells like somebody brought the good stuff. I'll find you in a few, babe."

With that, she just takes off, leaving me standing by the door alone. I laugh and shut the door behind me, taking a look around the huge house.

That's when I look up to see Jameson standing about halfway up the staircase, looking completely jaw dropping in a black button down shirt and fitted jeans.

The sight of him has my whole body buzzing with need, as our eyes meet.

Without a word, he nods for me to follow him up the stairs. My eyes instantly land on his sexy ass as I take the stairs one at a time.

My heart races with anticipation with each step I take, my mind spinning with all the possibilities of tonight.

Cole is most likely already up here waiting on me. I find it to be hot that Jameson is the one luring me to him.

Jameson waits for me to get upstairs, before he disappears into a room, confident that I'll follow.

He's right.

There's no controlling my body at this point. It wants what it wants and what it wants is one hot night with two hot men.

Just one night to feel them both without any worries of what's to come next.

Closing my eyes, I take a deep breath and slowly release it, before stepping into the room to see Cole sitting in a chair, holding a glass of liquor.

Jameson is standing in front of the fireplace and they both have their eyes on me, taking me in as if they're waiting for my reaction.

The room is dark, the mood seductive, giving me an idea of how this night is going to go.

Something about this moment tells me no words are needed.

They both want me and I want them to take me.

Standing up from the chair, Cole sets his glass down and walks over to the door, shutting it behind me.

I can feel his dark eyes burning into me as he looks me over in my dress, before pulling me against him and pressing his lips against my neck.

The feel of his lips sucking and nibbling have me moaning out and gripping his hair, wanting more.

That's when I look over Cole's shoulder to see Jameson push away from the fireplace and come at us, looking sexy and confident.

My breath escapes me the moment, his body closes in behind me, his hands slowly caressing my skin as he lowers my dress strap, while kissing my shoulder.

The feel of their lips on me, consume me, making my body ache for more than just their lips. I want to feel them on every inch of my body.

Closing my eyes, I lean my head back and allow the boys to undress me.

Their hands and lips are everywhere, making it impossible for me to catch my breath for a moment.

Within seconds, my dress is on the floor and Jameson is undoing my bra, while Cole is pulling my thong down my legs, his lips brushing down my body on the way.

My body is so sensitive from their touches that I find myself already coming close to reaching climax and it's just getting started.

Reaching for my hand, Cole places it on his chest, while slowly undoing the buttons of his shirt, moving my hand lower with each one he opens.

As if that isn't enough to drive me wild, Jameson takes my other hand, placing it on his belt, before whispering in my ear. "Undress us, Brooke."

After I undo Jameson's belt, he moves my hand over to Cole's belt, showing me they want me to undress Cole first.

As I'm working on Cole's jeans, Jameson wraps his arm around my neck, turning my head to the side so he can bite and suck my bottom lip.

I moan into his mouth and yank Cole's pants down his hips, feeling completely desperate to get these men naked at this point.

Once I get Cole's pants down to his ankles, he smirks and kicks his jeans to the side, before turning me around to face Jameson.

"You like feeling his lips on yours?" he questions against my ear, while moving me closer to his friend. "Kiss him and I'll kiss you . . ."

Before I can even think of what to say, Jameson has his hand tangled into the back of my hair, his lips slamming against mine.

Just like the other day, his kiss has my whole body igniting.

But as hard as I try to concentrate on how good Jameson's

lips feel, it's hard to think straight when I feel Cole spread my legs apart and run his tongue over my aching pussy.

Grabbing onto Jameson's strong shoulders, I moan into his mouth and shake in his arms as he holds me up.

I feel him smile against my mouth, before he bites me so hard that I scream out, not expecting it.

Somehow his teeth turn me on even more.

It also has Cole reacting, his mouth moving against me harder and faster as he slides his fingers in and out of me.

I can barely keep it together between Cole's mouth tasting me and Jameson moving my hands down his body so I can undress him.

Once Jameson is down to his briefs, I feel Cole pull his fingers out of me, before he bites my ass and then slaps it.

I'm standing here with two insanely half-naked men, unsure of how I'm still actually standing at this point.

Any girl in their right mind would've fangirled and fainted by now. Not me.

Confidence. I need to stay confident.

I stand still, breathing heavily as Cole walks around me, his eyes admiring me, before he stops in front of me and pulls me in for a kiss.

His kiss is deep and passionate as if to show me he doesn't think any less of me for wanting this.

It's almost as if he wants to show me he wants me more than Jameson does, yet, his kiss isn't quite doing the trick.

With Jameson's kiss . . . I felt more. It affected me more, but I fall into his mouth anyway, getting lost in the moment.

I'm not going to let their kisses distract me from what I want. What we all want right now.

While Cole is distracting me with his kiss, I feel Jameson wrap something around my eyes, securely tying it.

My first reaction is to scream because I've never been

blindfolded before, but the excitement of trying to guess who's doing what keeps me calm.

Cole pulls away from the kiss and before I can react, someone's hands are lifting me up and tossing me on the bed.

I land hard, gripping onto the blanket as I wait for what's to come next.

A small scream escapes my lips as hands unexpectedly grip my hips, pulling me to the edge of the bed.

I suck in a small breath and arch my back as I feel soft lips trail kisses up my thigh, getting extremely close to my pussy.

I expect whoever it is to keep moving, but they don't. It's a second set of lips that make their way to where I need to be kissed the most.

"Oh god . . ." I grab onto my hair and pull as I feel a tongue slide between my folds, before my clit is sucked between warm lips.

I can't tell at this point if it's Cole or Jameson, but one things for sure; it feels fantastic and I want more.

The tongue between my legs works with confidence, making my entire body scream out for release, while a second tongue runs up my thigh, teasing me.

Double the pleasure is definitely better. Oh. My. God.

"I'm so close . . ." I moan out. "It feels . . . ahhh. Keeping going. Keep going . . ."

I yank hard at my hair, before slamming my arms down onto the bed and moaning as I come undone for two sets of perfect lips.

The only sound I'm aware of after that is my heavy breathing as I feel a body hover above mine, lowering my hand down to the top of their boxer briefs.

My hands shake, barely able to keep in control as I lower the fabric down the body, feeling a thick erection rub against my arm.

Since they're so close in size and build it's impossible to know who's who right now.

Especially since they both decided not to wear their usual colognes. They planned this out. Every last detail to make sure to keep me guessing.

Hands grip my thighs, yanking them apart, before I hear what sounds like a condom wrapper.

I suck in a breath when I feel the head of a dick brush against my entrance, before slapping against my swollen clit.

"Ahhhh . . ." I grip the blanket and bite my bottom lip, sensations taking over me. Every single touch is intensified at the moment and I'm on the verge of going crazy.

A tongue swirls around my nipple, but it's hard to tell if it's from the person hovering above me or from the person beside the bed.

This is pure torture, trying to figure out who's about to enter me.

The tongue swirling around my nipple stops to bite it, right when I feel the intrusion of someone entering me.

It's thick and hard, making me cry out and dig my nails into the first thing I can touch.

As the body begins to move above me, taking me slow and deep, I get a feeling it's Cole on top of me.

Something about the way he's moving feels so familiar.

We've only had sex a few times, but I've paid very close attention to every last detail. Trust me on that.

He grips my thighs, digging his nails in as he leans in and kisses me, his pace quickening.

I know for sure now that it's Cole. His kiss is unmistakable.

As I'm moaning into his mouth, enjoying the feel of him inside of me, I feel Jameson take my hand and move it over his erection.

It has my heart hammering in my chest, knowing I'm touching his cock, while Cole is inside of me.

I've never felt something so damn hot and erotic in my life.

Jameson's hips begin to move, matching my movements and before I know it, Cole is pulling out of me and I feel the bed dip beside me as Jameson crawls in beside me.

Cole must me switching with him, because I no longer feel him next to me.

Strong hands grip my ass, pulling me across the bed to straddle a warm, firm body.

My heart is going crazy, knowing I'm about to finally have sex with Jameson. I'm about to feel him inside of me with his friend watching.

Holy fuck this is so dirty.

Tingles cover my body when I feel Jameson run his hands up my sides and arms as if he's taking this moment to admire the sight of me on top of him.

I find myself wishing I could see his eyes right now, but then again, maybe it's a good thing he can't see mine. I have no idea what they'd give away.

There's so many thoughts running through my head that I can't make sense of any of them. All I know is I'm desperate to feel him inside of me.

He's been torturing me for too long.

His hands slowly move back down my body again, landing on my hips, and before I can prepare myself, he's lifting me up and slowly lowering me down onto him, his thickness stretching me, making me want to cry out.

Right as a small noise escapes me, he grabs the back of my neck, pulling me down hard, so he can bite my bottom lip and push in as deeply as he can go.

His mouth moves around mine, capturing my small moans as he waits for me to adjust to his big size.

"Oh my god . . ." I whisper against his lips. "Please move, Jameson."

I feel him smile against my skin, before his mouth moves around to bite into my shoulder, right as he begins moving inside of me.

He brings me down hard with each thrust, both of his arms pulling me into him as roughly as he can, being sure he buries himself to the hilt each time.

It's as if he can't get deep enough, but he's still willing to try. He wants me to *feel* every single inch of him as he takes me slow and hard and I fucking love it.

His hands.

His mouth.

His body.

Everything about him is pure perfection.

Jameson continues to move inside me, his thrusts picking up, becoming rougher with each time I come down on top of him. I can feel his muscles flexing below my hands and I can't help but to run my fingers over every little dip, admiring the way his body moves.

It has me so turned on that I dig my nails into his firm chest and begin riding him hard and fast, unable to hold back anymore.

The sound of our bodies slapping together echoes throughout the room, turning me on even more.

It must work Jameson up too, because he pushes himself so deep inside of me that I scream out his name, giving away to Cole I know who's dick I'm taking.

"Fuck it," Jameson growls out, right before the fabric is yanked from my eyes and he positions my face so I'm looking down at him. "Look at me while I make you come."

My body trembles above him from his choice of words. I have no idea how this man has the power to make me come undone so easily.

Softly moaning, I dig my nails into his stomach muscles, keeping my eyes locked with his amber ones as he begins moving inside me again.

"Oh fuck," he moans out. "You feel better than I imagined, Brooke. Hold onto me."

His hands dig into my hips as he scoots his way off the bed, holding me up, as he stands to his feet.

I wrap my arms tightly around his neck, placing my forehead against his as he quickly slams me against the wall and begins fucking me hard and fast.

While keeping a steady rhythm, he pulls my arms away from his neck, capturing my wrists in his hands to pin them against the wall above me.

My body moves up the wall with each hard thrust, until I cry out my release, my body shaking in his strong arms as I come undone with him inside me.

With his eyes still on mine, he releases my wrists and grips the back of my neck, before lowering his lips to mine, catching my remaining moans as he growls out from his own release.

We're both breathing heavily, him just holding me, until Cole comes up from beside us and pulls me into his arms.

That's when I remember Cole hasn't come yet.

Raising me up, he lowers my aching pussy onto his dick and begins slowly moving inside me, while walking across the room to slam me against the door.

His lips and teeth graze my body as his movements pick up, until I'm screaming out his name just as I did with Jameson not even five minutes ago.

Growling out, he backs us away from the wall, positioning us back on the bed, but with me on top of him this time.

I let out a surprised gasp when I feel Jameson move in behind me, lifting my ass up to rub the head of his dick against me.

He must notice me stiffen up, because he wraps his arm around the front of my neck, pulling me back to whisper in my ear. "Relax and let us take care of you."

Cole stills his movement, gently massaging the side of my face as Jameson slowly enters my ass, doing his best not to hurt me.

It hurts, yet feels so fucking good as he eases himself inside of me inch by inch, until he's finally as far as he can go.

I moan out and arch my back, reaching my arms behind me to grip the back of Jameson's head as he begins thrusting in and out of my ass, while Cole falls into rhythm, taking my pussy at the same time.

Their hands are all over my body, both men filling me completely as I grip on for dear life and let them take me.

"Oh shit . . ." My grip on Jameson becomes tighter as he grips my throat from behind as he grinds into me, burying himself even deeper.

It's as if Jameson always pulls out, just in time for Cole to thrust in.

I can't take this. I feel as if I'm about to pass out from the pleasure that's overwhelming me.

It's too much.

"I'm about to come," I whisper. "Keep going."

Both boys keep going, until I'm screaming out from my orgasm, their hands and bodies holding me up so I don't collapse.

After a few seconds, I feel Jameson kiss the side of my neck, before he slowly pulls out of me, giving Cole room to finish.

Cole pulls me down to him, his lips capturing mine as he pushes me down onto his dick one last time, holding me still as he comes into the condom.

These boys have me so exhausted that all I can do is go limp in his arms and breath heavily into his neck.

We stay still for a few moments, us both fighting to catch our breath, before he lifts me off him and lowers me down to the bed.

His kiss is rough and deep, before he smiles against my lips.

"You can shower down the hall and clean us off you. I want you with me tonight."

"Thank you," is all I can manage to say as I grab the shirt Jameson holds out for me. "Why is it so quiet downstairs?"

"I asked Rowdy to move the party to his place after you arrived. Karson is safe in his hands." Jameson's eyes land on my lips as he runs a hand through his hair. "You and Cole can have the guest room tonight since it's so late. I'll shower down the hall and let you have my bathroom."

"Nah, that's okay," Cole speaks up. "You take your bathroom and I'll take Brooke down the hall so we can both shower."

Jameson just nods his head, while reaching for his jeans and slipping them on.

Tons of emotions swarm through me the second we leave Jameson alone in his room to shower.

By the time Cole and I are done and getting comfy in Jameson's guest room, it's just past two in the morning. That means we were in Jameson's room for a good two hours, while the boys took turns with me.

I'm definitely feeling it now. My whole body is sore.

Cole falls asleep right away, him holding me tightly in his arms, but I can't seem to shut my mind off long enough to fall asleep myself.

Why is it that Jameson is the only thing I can think about now? Being with him felt so much better than I could've ever expected and something in his eyes tells me he felt it too.

A part of me wishes it were his bed I'm in right now instead of in here with Cole . . .

CHAPTER FOURTEEN

Jameson

I T'S NEARLY FOUR IN THE morning and I still haven't been able to force myself to get some sleep.

My brain won't shut the fuck up to the fact that Cole and Brooke are asleep, together, in my guest room across the hall.

After my promise to Cole that I was done pursuing Brooke after tonight, offering them a place to sleep just seemed like the *best friend* thing to do.

It's something I would've been okay with in the past, yet something is eating away at me, making me want to walk into the guest room and carry Brooke back to *my* bed.

Growling out, I slam the empty bottle of Jack down and run my hands through my hair in frustration.

I'm fucking pissed at myself right now. Pissed that I'm allowing whatever the hell these emotions are to consume me and keep my head spinning.

Tonight, wasn't supposed to feel this way. Being inside Brooke wasn't supposed to make me feel as if we were the only two in that bedroom.

And I sure as hell wasn't supposed to want to cover her up with my blanket and then kick Cole out so she could spend the night in my arms, while I took her over and over again, until her body couldn't handle me.

The way she screamed my name and dug her nails into me when I was inside her spoke to my heart and not only my dick. She put so much emotion into it.

"Fuuuck!"

"Everything okay in here?"

My heart speeds up as I look toward the doorway to see Brooke standing there, looking extremely sexy in my t-shirt.

She's looking at me as if she wants to come in my room, but isn't sure if it's a good idea or not.

It only makes me want to throw her back onto my bed, strip her out of my shirt, and spend the whole night pleasuring every inch of her body.

That can't happen so . . .

"Just can't sleep," I admit. "Having the same problem?"

She shakes her head and walks into my room, taking a seat on the floor, in front of the fireplace.

I sit back in my chair and watch her as she just watches the flames dance in the darkness.

I'm intrigued by her beauty as she gets lost in thought for a moment.

"This is the first time I've spent the night with a guy in a very long time. I'm not used to sharing a bed. I don't know . . ."

I find myself wanting to ask questions about her and get to know her even though I probably shouldn't with what's going on in my head right now. It's not my place to ask this, but I ask anyway.

"How long has it been?"

She looks over at me when I stand from my chair to take a seat beside her on the floor. We're close, but I make sure not too close where I won't be able to resist the temptation to touch her and taste her lips again.

"About two years. My ex decided to take off after my mother got sick and passed away. No goodbye. No nothing. Just quit returning my calls. He ended up being a real dick."

"He's a fucking piece of shit. That's what he is for doing that to you." My blood boils hearing that her ex was heartless enough to leave her alone as such a shitty time in her life. She doesn't deserve that hurt. "He's an asshole that doesn't deserve your time. Trust me. A real man would never abandon a woman when she needs him the most."

"That's what Karson's been telling me since he ditched me. I guess he couldn't handle my depression or the struggle I was going through to keep my mother's café going at the time." She pauses and starts fingering the bottom of my shirt she's wearing. "After she passed, I tried to keep it running smoothly, but after shutting it down for four weeks to grieve, the business just wasn't the same when I reopened it. I ended up selling it to pay off funeral and burial expenses and used the rest to pay off the mortgage on my mother's house."

I feel my heart ache for the pain she went through and knowing some douchebag decided to abandon her pisses me the fuck off. Makes me want to choke him out.

But I need to keep my cool and remind myself she's not *mine* to protect.

"What was the name of your mother's café?"

"*Little Suzie's Café.* She opened it when I was just ten. I spent a lot of time playing in the back while she worked."

My heart stops when she says the name. It's been at least three years since I've been there, but I had no idea Suzie passed away.

She didn't seem sick back when I used to stop in there each week. "I used to go there every Sunday for Suzie's famous cherry pie. Shit. I had no idea." I stand up and begin pacing the room as emotions build up inside me. "I'm so sorry to hear about her passing. She was a sweet lady. Always good to me. A little feisty when someone pissed her off, but I liked her."

"You knew my mother?" She laughs as if remembering something. "You must've been on her good side. Be thankful for that."

"I was." I laugh when a certain memory of her comes to mind. "I would've hated to be on her bad side. I witnessed her make a grown man cry before. He didn't really cry, but shit, he came close. I'll never forget the ass chewing she gave him for disrespecting her. I was about to throw him out myself, until Suzie showed me she didn't need my help."

This causes Brooke to let loose and laugh so hard that I find myself smiling as I watch her. "I got my feisty side from her, so you might want to make sure you never piss me off."

I clench my jaw and turn away. "I can't make any promises."

The room is silent for a few moments, before she speaks again. "What about you? Any family?"

The thought of my father is enough to have me searching the room for my spare bottle of Jack. I know it's here somewhere. *Shit.*

Once I find it, I pour a glass and stand in front of the fireplace. "Yeah . . . a little sister named Kai. My mother died when I was a baby and my father took off seven years ago, as soon as I reached the legal age for me to be on my own." I look around the room. His old room and it only makes me hate the man more. "He left me this fucking house as if it would make up for him abandoning me. Haven't seen him since and don't really care to. He was a shitty father and that's why my sister pretty much grew up at her friend's house."

Her eyes look sad as they watch me tilt back the bottle. "I'm sorry to hear that. He sounds like a dick."

"Yeah, he is."

The last thing I want to do is think about my shitty childhood or the fact I want to comfort *her* right now. My pain is nothing compared to hers.

Too many emotions are not a good thing right now.

But I can't help but to wonder why she's living in a crappy apartment building when she used money from the café to pay off her mother's mortgage.

"Why don't you live in your mother's house?" I ask before I can stop myself.

Brooke let's out a small breath and turns away from me as if she doesn't want me to see her get emotional. "Before my mother died, she was in the middle of remodeling the living room and dining room floors. The house was left a total mess and I just couldn't find it in me to stay there after she died, knowing she never got to finish. Looking at the mess would've reminded me too much. I meant to hire someone to finish the work later, but not a lot of money was left after I paid off all the expenses."

My breathing picks up as Brooke stands to her feet and walks over to stand next to me. Her blue eyes meet mine and as hard as I try to look away, I can't.

A strong urge to pull her against me and kiss her pain away takes over and I find myself fighting with everything in me not to act on it.

We still somehow get within just a few inches of each other, until I find myself breathing above her lips.

Just as I think of something to say, Cole appears in the doorway, tapping the wall to get our attention. "You guys good in here?" He runs a hand down his face and watches as I back away from Brooke and cuss under my breath. It's hard to mistake the worry in his eyes from seeing us so close just now. "I woke up and you were gone. It's late. Let's let Jameson sleep. You can talk to me if you can't sleep."

Brooke takes a few quick breaths and backs away herself as if she's just woken up from a trance. "Goodnight, Jameson" she whispers.

"Goodnight. Thanks for the talk."

Cole's eyes meet mine after Brooke leaves the room. It looks as if he has something to say, but brushes it off. "Goodnight, man."

I nod my head and hold the bottle of Jack up. "Night."

Once I'm alone again, I spend the next hour, staring at the fire, while replaying Brooke's story over and over in my head.

It seems to be bothering me that the only reason she's not staying in her home is because her mother's work was left unfinished.

I can't get that shit out of my head. It's eating at me.

All I can think of is how I want to help her . . .

CHAPTER FIFTEEN

Brooke

IT'S BEEN ALMOST A WEEK since my extremely *hot* night with Cole and Jameson and I still haven't been able to stop replaying it in my head, repeatedly.

It was the single most intense moment of my life, having both of their hands and mouths all over me, touching and tasting me.

The feeling is still teasing and taunting me, making it impossible to forget the sensory overload I experienced that night.

Seriously, you try going to work with those images consuming you and see how well you can function. It's close to impossible, making it extremely difficult to do my job.

Hell, I'm surprised Ben hasn't given me the boot yet.

I can't even count the times Karson has had to snap my ass back to reality and remind me that I have a damn job to do.

I seriously owe her big time for being here for me, because I have no idea how I'd be able to think straight for longer than ten minutes, without her distracting me and pulling me from my torturous mind.

It's not even just the threesome that's been screwing with me and causing me to get lost in my head. There's something much bigger that's been taking over and consuming me.

Jameson . . .

I've been thinking a lot about how being with Jameson made me feel that night.

The way he kissed me and moved inside of me with so much meaning, felt like so much more than just a fun experience he was just a part of. He made me feel as if we were the only two in the room.

Cole failed to make me feel that way. I was aware of Jameson's presence when Cole was inside of me, the *entire* time.

I don't think I'm meant to be missing Jameson the way I am, but I can't push him out of my mind or stop wondering when I'll see him again.

I've seen Cole almost every day now and every single time, I hope that *maybe* Jameson will be close behind, but he never is.

I'm not sure what I expected to happen *after* our little three-some, but I guess I hoped he'd still be around. It's as if I've gotten used to the possibility of him just showing up or texting me out of nowhere as if it's become the normal for us.

And now . . . nothing.

The way is absence is affecting me is confusing the hell out of me.

"You're doing it again . . ."

"Doing what?" I shove my phone aside and try to convince myself I haven't been waiting to hear from Jameson. Fooling my-self is harder than I thought. "I was checking the time. That's all."

Karson flashes me a sympathy smile and reaches for my phone, shoving it into her pocket. "It's staying in my pants for safe keeping. You just have to make it through thirty more minutes. Give your phone a rest and take care of your thirsty customers. *I have a song to sing that might cheer you up.*"

I smile and roll my eyes as Karson rushes up to the stage to take over the mic.

It's her day off, yet she chose to spend my entire shift here, hanging out and singing me random songs every time the bar becomes quiet.

It's a Thursday evening so that's often. Too often. Trust me. At this point, I'd *pay* Ben to shut down the bar for the night, just so I wouldn't have to listen to Karson sing one more damn song.

Too bad that's not an option.

I about die when she speaks into the mic and points to me, right as I'm in the middle of making a drink for a customer. "This song is for my freaky deaky little friend over there. I so envy you."

My face turns red as *3* by Britney Spears begins playing over the speakers and eyes around the room seem to gravitate toward me as random people cheer and congratulate me as if I've just won the lottery or some shit.

"That little bitch." I run my hands over my face and repeatedly tell myself to let Karson keep breathing once this song ends.

"What are best friends for?" My boss appears next to me, watching Karson with a huge smile. It's as if he's amused by this. Not that I expect any different from him. He's a little crazy his damn self. I wouldn't be surprised if he joined her on stage just to embarrass me more.

"Embarrassment, apparently. At least mine is, anyway. Can you make her stop?"

"Can anyone make her do anything?" He lifts a brow. "Besides, there's nothing to be embarrassed about," he says, while grabbing for a water. "You seem to be the luckiest person in the room tonight."

With that, he walks away, while mouthing the lyrics.

I shake my head and shoot Karson an evil glare, before quickly sliding the two cocktails to the lady in front of me and grabbing the money from her hand.

I'm pretty sure she's about to question Karson's song choice, so I take off before she can even move her curious lips.

Even though Karson is a pain in my ass, I can't help but to smile as I stand back and watch her sing. This song is fucking ridiculous and she looks even more ridiculous singing it.

If she was looking to make me smile . . . it worked.

After Karson's song, I begin cleaning up, getting the bar prepared for Ariel's shift.

Lucky for me, she shows up fifteen minutes early, eager to start her shift and kick me out for the night.

So I meet Karson outside in the parking lot and jump into her car expecting her to head toward my apartment, but am surprised when I realize where's she actually headed.

My heart beats faster, the closer we get to the building.

"What do you think you're doing?" I question, while looking out the window with wide eyes. "Please tell me we're not going to *Club Reckless*. I'll see Cole when he gets off work."

"And what about Jameson? Isn't he the one you *really* want to see?"

I shake my head, denying the truth. Why does she keep bringing Jameson up? This will be the third time this week and it's driving me crazy. "There's no reason for me to see Jameson. What was supposed to happen, happened, and now it's over. I'm talking to Cole and Jameson is probably talking to someone else. That's how it's meant to be. So, can you stop bringing him up, please?"

"What if that's not how it's meant to be? Who told you that bullshit anyway?"

I shoot my head in her direction and release a disappointed breath, remembering Jameson's words. "Jameson warned me not to fall for him before we even had sex. He made it clear that if I fall for anyone it needed to be Cole, not him."

Karson quickly parks and shifts the car into park. "Well, shit changes. Let's go inside, order a drink and have a little fun."

Even though my head is screaming at me to tell her no and take a damn Uber home if needed, I follow her past Rowdy and into the club anyway.

I'm a little surprised she didn't stop to flirt or tell me to go in by myself so she could hang with Rowdy. She just eye fucked him a little and kept moving. It's as if she's desperate to get me inside. I don't get her sometimes.

We're here just long enough to order drinks and hit the dance-floor, when I look over and spot Jameson, standing with his arms crossed.

My heart instantly skips a beat, making me choke on my drink and fight to catch my breath through my coughing fit.

Why does he have to be so damn beautiful?

My heart almost can't handle him.

Literally . . .

"You okay?" Karson slaps my back as if I'm a child. "I can't have you dying on me before we even get a chance to dance. Breathe . . ."

I nod my head and cough up the last bit, hoping like hell Karson doesn't notice my reason for choking and about dying. "I'm good. You can stop slapping me now."

She laughs. "You sure?"

"Positive," I say, while still eyeing Jameson from across the room, completely distracted by his presence. "No, I don't need a new one . . ."

"What are you talking about?"

My vison of Jameson gets blocked when Karson steps in front of me, most likely testing me.

If she is, I totally failed, because I instantly move my body to the left, standing on my tippy toes just to get another glimpse of him.

"I knew it." She steps out of the way and turns behind her to look at Jameson. "I spotted him a few seconds ago. Was wondering when you would."

I keep staring hard, as if Jameson is supposed to magically know I'm here and look in my direction.

"Doesn't matter." I take a sip of my drink, being extra careful this time. "I'm not here for him."

Just then, Jameson looks my direction, his eyes landing on me.

His whole body stiffens, his jaw flexing as he looks me over, taking me in. I can almost see a softness in his eyes as if he's happy to see me, but then, just like that, he quickly pulls his eyes away, as if he didn't just see me standing here.

It hurts.

I feel it in my chest as disappointment washes over me, reminding me I'm meant to fall for Cole.

Not Jameson.

Maybe this is his way of reminding me just that and it sucks . . . royally.

"He's probably just distracted," Karson says from beside me. She nudges my arm and smiles. "Let's just dance and have some fun, okay. He's in a difficult position. Don't hold it against him."

I nod my head and whisper, "Yeah, okay."

As hard as I try to have fun with Karson and forget about Jameson ignoring me as if I don't even exist to him anymore, I can't.

It's eating at me, making it hard to have any fun. My fucking heart hurts right now.

And it's all my fault. Jameson warned me not to fall for him and I did anyway . . .

CHAPTER SIXTEEN

Jameson

BROOKE WALKED IN TEN MINUTES ago, and I've been fighting like hell to keep my eyes off her, but it's impossible. I feel like a complete dick for turning away from her when our eyes met, but I knew if I allowed myself to keep looking, that I'd end up with her in my damn arms.

That's the last place she's meant to be.

Since then, I've been stealing glances of her from across the room, every chance I get, in hopes she won't notice me watching her.

Hell, I shouldn't even be looking in her direction, knowing Cole is just downstairs and could come up at any second.

But the truth is, I haven't been able to stop thinking about her since she left my bedroom last week.

Visions of me sinking between her legs have been haunting me, reminding me of how good it felt to be inside her, both mentally and physically.

I was right, fucking Cole's girl was *exactly* what it took for me to get over him fucking me over with Katie, except now . . . now I can't get over *his* girl.

Cole knows it too. I'm positive of that shit.

That's *exactly* why I need to make Brooke believe I don't want her.

Things with Cole are back to normal and I need to keep them that way before I destroy our friendship for good.

If I went after what I really wanted, Cole would hate me forever and we'd probably never speak again.

"Lil' cousin. Damn, you're getting ripped. Chasing down assholes has really paid off."

Releasing a slow breath, I pull my eyes away from Brooke and turn around to the vision of Stefan's cocky face. He's dressed in his fancy, expensive suit, looking me over as if he's better than me.

I haven't seen his ass in over six months, so I guess you can say I'm a little fucking surprised to see him.

The asshole isn't really my cousin, but since my sister practically grew up at his house with his sister, we became a forced family sort of.

"Stefan," I say stiffly. "You always have the shittiest timing."

He points to himself. "Who me? Nah." Grinning, he slaps my chest and then pulls me in for a tight hug, wrapping his arm around my neck so he can talk in my ear. "Got a minute? I have a favor to ask you."

Pushing away from his grip, I head toward the back room, knowing he'll follow if he needs me badly enough.

His favors are never good for me and he's lucky I'm even giving him a chance after the last one he asked of me.

Walking into the back room, I close the door behind us and lean against the front of the desk, crossing my arms over my chest.

"I'm probably not going to like whatever words come out

of your mouth, but ask, since I know you will anyway. I'm a little busy. So, make it quick."

He runs a hand through his blonde, perfectly styled hair, before pulling out his wallet and flipping through the bills. "I need you to keep an eye on my girl for me. She wants to have a little fun tonight, but I can't stay. Got some other shit to take care of."

"Put your fucking money away. I have my own cash, asshole. I just choose not to flaunt it around like you." I push the ear piece further into my ear, when I hear Cole's voice come through, asking me to come watch the poker room for him so he can take a quick break. "And hurry this shit up. Like I said . . . I have work to do."

"Alright, cousin, shit. I'm only asking you this because I need to keep all the assholes away from Abby since I can't be here to watch her and well . . . security is sort of your thing." He looks me over, taking in my size. "She likes to dance, so I know dickheads will be lining up to grind their little dicks all over her. You have Katie so I know you'll keep yours in your pants."

He's a clueless asshole. But I'm not getting into Katie or Brooke with him right now. All I want is to get this conversation over with.

"Since when the fuck have you given a shit about anyone other than yourself, for you to have a girl for longer than a week?"

Standing tall, he fixes his tie with a smug smile. "Since some crazy as hell woman rode my dick so hard that the headboard busted my wall. I want to make sure I'm still getting that treatment after tonight. I can't have some prince fucking charming swooping in while I'm not here, stealing her away. We've only been messing around for a month, but hell, I might just keep this one around for a while. After I'm done taking care of some other business."

"You're an asshole. You know that, right?" I uncross my arms and stand up straight, surprised at what he's asking of me.

The guy's a total douche that can't keep a girl to save his life. And before tonight, he hasn't wanted to.

"I'm pretty sure you can handle my girl for me, right?" He slaps my chest and begins backing up toward the door. "I'll bring her inside. Let me go get her."

"Never fucking said . . ."

Before I can respond to the cocky bastard, he rushes out of the room, getting lost in the crowd.

The last thing I want right now is to take care of anyone else's fucking girl. I've already gotten myself into a mess with Cole's.

But apparently, this idiot plans to leave her in my hands anyway. He's just lucky I can't say no to making sure she's safe. On top of me caring about a woman's safety; it's my job.

I won't be doing it for his wellbeing. That's for damn sure.

"Fuck, I'm going to lose my shit tonight."

Not even two minutes later, I spot Stefan walking back toward me, guiding some beautiful blonde chick through the club.

He practically pushes her into my arms.

"Abby, meet my cousin Jameson. If you need anything at all, find him. Don't trust any other asshole and don't forget his pretty face."

Abby smiles up at me, giving me eyes that could only mean trouble. I can't deal with this kind of shit right now. "I definitely won't forget that face."

Frustration takes over as I begin looking around, wondering where Brooke is. The last thing I want is for her to think some other girl is here for me.

I want to make it clear I'm staying away from her and letting Cole have what he wants, but I'm not a heartless bastard that plans to use another girl to get that point across.

"I'll be downstairs for fifteen minutes," I say, while backing away from his girl. "Have her stay in this area and I'll be back when I can. You might want to at least stay until I get back."

Before Stefan can respond, I rush off to the back, ready to get as far away from up here as I can.

Everything upstairs screams trouble for my ass.

Just as I'm opening the door to the game room downstairs, I hear shouting from above, letting me know a fight has either broken out or will shortly be breaking out.

"Fucking shit. Stefan better not be getting his ass kicked already."

Slamming the door shut, I run up the stairs, taking them two at a time.

Once I reach the top, I push my way through the crowd, shouting for people to get out of my way, so I can break up the fight.

Relief washes through me when I see that it's not Stefan. He may be an asshole, but he's sort of family. I'd feel like shit, not being around to stop him from getting his ass kicked.

I've seen him in a fight before and trust me, he fights like he looks: pretty.

Rushing over to the bigger of the two guys, I pull him away from the guy on the floor, slamming him down at my feet.

"Fuck," he chokes out, while trying to see who just took him down to his back.

I hold him down by his neck, looking up right as Rowdy appears out of nowhere to grab the other guy and restrain him.

Getting the big dude back up to his feet, I wrap my arm around his neck from behind, and start pushing him toward the exit door.

"What the fuck are you doing?" he yells at me. "Get off me, prick."

Holding him tighter, I lean down by his ear and growl. "Don't fight me, because trust me, I won't be as easy as your little friend was. I will knock you on your ass and trust me, you won't be getting back up for a while."

I fight to restrain him, but get distracted by Brooke watching me as I pass by her and Karson.

She's watching me hard, as if she's either impressed or turned on by seeing me overpower such a big guy.

It's completely fucking distracting, trying to figure out what's running through her head right now.

Locking my eyes with hers, I seem to focus on her, instead of keeping my arm firm around the guy's neck.

He takes my arm loosening, as his opportunity to push my arm away and swing at me.

That has me turning away from Brooke and grabbing the guy by the neck, slamming him back down to the ground.

I hear him release a hard breath this time, before he starts coughing and fighting to catch his breath.

Smirking, I get down in his face and squeeze his throat. "Better luck, next time, buddy. Now get the fuck up."

I release his throat and grab onto his shirt and jeans, pulling him back up to his feet, and dragging him toward the door.

Rowdy already has someone driving his guy out of the parking lot, so he meets me at the door, handling him from there.

Breathing heavily, I walk back into the club, stopping to roll up my sleeves and undo a few buttons to cool off.

As I'm making my way through the crowd, Stefan passes me, stopping first, to let me know to handle any asshole who even talks to Abby, the same way I handled that douche.

Right after he walks away, his girl rushes over to me, hanging on my ass as if she's turned on by what I just did.

And of course, Brooke's eyes land on me right as she wraps her arm around my neck and pulls me against her, rubbing her body against mine.

There's no mistaking the hurt and jealously on Brooke's face, right before she turns away and slams back her drink, emptying it.

Just fucking great . . .

Making sure not to be too rough with Abby, I push her away

from me and remove her arm from around my neck. "Can't. I have work to do."

"Oh . . . come on." Smiling, she runs her finger down my chest and abs, before looping it into the front of my belt and pulling on me again. "Stefan doesn't dance. I'm pretty sure he wouldn't mind if you danced with me instead. There's no harm in an innocent dance."

I hear Cole speaking into the earpiece again, attempting to get my attention, so I yank her hand away, getting angry now.

Between Brooke probably thinking I'm into Abby and Cole rushing my ass to get downstairs, I'm close to losing my shit and going off on the next person who pisses me off.

"I'll be downstairs. Get a drink from the bar and tell Violet it's on me."

I take off, making my way back downstairs before she can attempt to grab me again.

Cole is waiting by the door when I open it, giving me a pissed off look. "What the hell, man. I've had to piss for over thirty minutes now."

"Got slowed down by Stefan stopping in," I say annoyed. "Sorry, man."

He walks past me and begins making his way upstairs.

As much as I hate the idea of him touching Brooke, I figure she's probably here to see him anyway. He might as well know.

"Brooke and Karson are upstairs in section B."

Cole stops walking and turns around to look at me. Worry flashes in his eyes for a quick second, before he just nods and walks away.

Fuck this night. I'm so damn pissed at myself right now, that all I want to do is throw my fist through a wall.

So much for getting back at Cole. All I did was fuck myself up . . .

CHAPTER SEVENTEEN

Brooke

SEEING THAT GIRL PUT HER hands all over Jameson and rub her body against him as if he was hers to touch, made me want to pull her away from him.

A pang of jealousy had me squeezing my glass tightly and finishing off the rest of my drink in a hurry, before I could even consider doing something so ridiculous.

I admit, I've never felt so strong of a jealousy in my entire life. Not even when girls used to flirt with Jeremy, back when we were dating, did I feel what I'm feeling right this second.

Not even close.

The bad thing is, Jameson isn't even mine to be jealous over. I have absolutely no right to be upset right now. But when I saw that hot blonde put her hands on him, my heartbeat sped up, beating so hard I could hear it in my ears and my stomach twisted into knots.

I don't know why it was so unexpected, seeing him with someone else. He's free to be with anyone he wants. We aren't together, but doesn't mean it made seeing him with another woman hurt any less.

It's an image I want to erase from my mind as soon as possible and forget I ever saw it.

"What the hell is wrong with me?" I push past Karson and make my way over to the bar to order another drink.

I'm not thinking straight. I *shouldn't* be as upset as I am and I *shouldn't* want to slam back another drink to forget Jameson all together, but apparently, my heart isn't getting the memo.

It's still beating out of my chest this very second, imagining him taking her home and giving her what he gave me just last week.

His hands and tongue on her body as he takes her to his bed and has sex with her, making her moan in all the ways he made me moan.

The thought makes me want to scream.

I feel Karson come up behind me and place her hand on my arm to get my attention, right as the bartender pushes my much needed drink in front of me.

"Are you okay? I haven't seen you this red and worked up in a long time."

Ignoring Karson's question, I grab for some cash and attempt to give it to the bartender, but she shakes her head and pushes my hand away. "Apparently, your money isn't needed here. Enjoy." With that, she winks and rushes off to help someone else.

For some reason, I have a feeling my free drinks here, are due to Jameson. All that does is gives me more reason to think about him.

Thinking about him *needs* to stop.

"I'm so damn screwed."

"Are you going to talk to me or are you going to have this conversation with yourself, Brooke?"

I take a huge drink of my cocktail and finally turn around to face Karson, prepared to let it all spill. There's no point in even trying to hide it from her anymore. Besides, I'm pretty sure she's figured it out by now.

She's been my best friend for as long as I can remember. She's always the first to know how and what I'm feeling.

"I think I'm falling for Jameson," I breathe out. "I can't stop thinking about him. I just can't and I feel stupid for feeling this way, when he clearly doesn't feel the same. What kind of girl goes and falls for the best friend of the guy she's talking to? I'm a bitch."

I begin pushing my way through the room, eager to get some air. Being in this club, has me feeling as if I'm suffocating. I can't breathe and I'm pretty sure you can see sweat trickling down my forehead by now. I need to get away.

Far away from Jameson and far away from Cole, before he realizes I'm here and catches on to my little breakdown.

"I know I shouldn't be feeling this way about him, but I can't help it, Karson. I should be thinking about Cole. I should be wondering where he is, but I'm not. Cole is who I should *want* to be with."

"And that's fine," Karson says, while stopping me from walking out the door. "It's okay to feel for someone other than Cole. Just because you liked him first, doesn't mean you're supposed to be with him. You and Cole never set up any kind of rules or even discussed making it exclusive. You need to calm down and breathe."

"But Cole cares about me." I take a deep breath and slowly release it, while fighting to gather my thoughts. Cole has been making it very clear lately he's beginning to fall for me and it's been scaring the shit out of me for some reason. "I care about him too, but . . . something with Jameson feels different. With Cole, I didn't care if he wasn't interested in attachments in the beginning. I was okay with the idea of it never turning into anything permanent. Why does it hurt to think I'll never get a chance to touch or kiss Jameson again? Why does the idea of him being with another girl kill me?"

Karson is just about to open her mouth to speak, when Cole approaches us from the side, looking tired and out of breath as if he's been fighting his way over to find me.

He flashes me a grateful smile and pulls me against him for a kiss.

His mouth is soft and warm, making it easy to fall into him, but I can't seem to get lost in his kiss like I did in the beginning.

All I keep thinking about is how it felt when Jameson used to kiss me like this.

He must notice my uneasiness, because he pulls away and runs his hand through my hair, looking concerned. "I missed you today. Was hoping you'd stop in so I could see you."

I force a smile and try my best to pretend I'm not thinking about his friend. I just hope I can pull it off.

"Karson surprised me by coming here after my shift," I explain. "My plan was to just see you after you got off tonight."

I can feel his heart hammering inside his chest as he rubs his thumb over my bottom lip and smiles. "I'll still come over tonight. Maybe I'll just crash at your apartment and we can get breakfast in the morning."

Guilt rushes through me at the realization that making plans with Cole isn't what I want or need right now. The thought of him sleeping in my bed has me trying to come up with an excuse to tell him no.

How am I supposed to lay next to Cole, when all I can think about is Jameson?

I close my eyes and lean my face into his touch, trying to come up with the words I need right now.

He's been so gentle and caring lately, that I hate to give him any reason to be upset.

"Sorry, big guy. Tonight, is a girl's only slumber party. That's why we're here now," Karson says, surprising me. "Get your few minutes in and say goodnight, babe."

Cole smiles down at me, before leaning in and pressing his lips against mine again. "Sounds like you have a fun night ahead of you."

My eyes meet his caring ones and a genuine smile takes over as he pulls me against him and wraps his hands into the back of my hair. It's almost enough to make me stop thinking about Jameson, but it only works for a split second.

It's going to take a lot more than I thought to make me forget about how it felt to be with him.

"Things with Karson are always *entertaining*." I catch Karson grinning at me from my peripheral vision. "Are you stuck down-stairs again tonight?"

He nods his head. "Yeah. Jameson is holding down my spot right now . . ." he trails off as if he's trying to figure out if he should say what he's thinking. "He's the one that told me you were here. Were you guys spending time together before he came down to get me? He looked pretty uptight about something?"

"No." The word stings, reminding me of how harsh it felt when he just ignored me. "He didn't even say hi."

Relief washes over Cole's face, before he begins massaging my cheekbone with his thumb. "I should get back downstairs. It's probably best if you stay away from Jameson for now. Just until the events of last week isn't so fresh in our minds. Okay?"

Tell me about it. It feels as if it just happened yesterday and everything about that night is still hitting me hard.

"Yeah . . . I agree."

"Good." Leaning in, he gently pulls my bottom lip between his teeth, giving me a soft nibble, before sweeping his tongue over the spot he just bit.

I can feel him smile against my mouth, before he crushes his lips to mine, pulling me as close to him as humanly possible.

He's kissing me as if he doesn't want to let me go. It's enough to have me wrapping my arms around his neck and getting lost in the moment.

It's when the moment is over that I open my eyes to see Jameson talking to the blonde chick, while staring hard in our direction.

The intensity of his stare has my heart going crazy in my chest.

He looks just about as jealous and pissed off as I felt when I first saw him with the blonde chick he's now with, *again*.

Apparently, she *is* here for him since she's still practically on his ass.

"I thought Jameson was downstairs?" I question in a shaky voice.

Cole releases his grip on me to turn behind him. "Rev showed up a second ago and took over downstairs. Looks like we'll both be upstairs now for the rest of the night."

This is the first time I've been in the same room with them since that night. If it felt like I was suffocating before, I'm definitely drowning, barely able to breathe now.

"Oh . . ." is all I can manage as Jameson looks me over, taking me in as I stand here, still pressed against Cole's body. "I think me and Karson are about to take off and start our girl's night. It's already getting late and . . ."

"We have a TV show to binge watch," Karson jumps in. "About sexy vampires and werewolves. There's twenty-three episodes a season so we need to jump in." Karson flashes Cole a smile and pulls me away from him. "Like now."

"Alright . . ." Cole looks amused as Karson wraps her arm in mine. "You ladies enjoy your vampires and werewolves then."

I try my hardest not to look back over in Jameson's direction, but I can't help but want to see if he's still with blondie.

He is and the idea of leaving him here with her makes my chest ache.

"I'll text you tomorrow after work." I pull my eyes away from

Jameson, and set them back on Cole, before he can figure out I'm staring at his friend like a fool. "Gotta go before Karson drags me out of here."

Before Cole can manage to say anything, Karson is dragging me away and out the door.

Rowdy is standing there with his clipboard, but quickly looks our direction when Karson screams, "Holy shit!"

"Both the boys upstairs now?" Rowdy questions, while setting his clipboard down and pulling a joint from his pocket.

"Yup." Karson watches as Rowdy lights up his joint and passes it to me.

"You need this. It'll help you relax." He turns back to Karson and flashes her a sexy smile. "Just hurry to your car before Mason chews my ass out and accuses me of smoking at the door again."

Ignoring them both, I walk away and quickly take a few hits, hoping like hell Rowdy is right.

Relaxing is what I desperately need to do at the moment.

Why the hell did I get myself into this mess . . .

CHAPTER EIGHTEEN

Jameson

S EEING BROOKE KISS COLE HURT like hell and made me want to rip his fucking head off.

I can't keep my thoughts straight and telling myself that backing off is the right thing to do, doesn't seem to be working at the moment.

All I want to do is show up at her house, throw her against the wall and put my mouth and hands all over her.

I want to erase Cole's touch from her and make sure *mine* is the only one she *feels*.

There's only one thing I can do to distract myself from doing that now that the night is over and Stefan finally picked up his girl, freeing me up.

"Hey, man." Cole comes jogging across the parking lot, right as I straddle my bike. It's taking a lot for me not to want to kill him. "I'm heading to Rowdy's to drink and chill. You coming?"

"Nah . . ." I slide my helmet on and start my bike. "I need

some air. I'll just catch you guys tomorrow."

"Yup," Cole says stiffly, while backing away. "Have fun, *brother*."

From the coldness in Cole's voice, I'm guessing he assumes getting some air involves Brooke.

Lucky for him, it doesn't.

I've been working on a little something for the last week to keep my ass distracted.

What happens when I'm done could be a good thing or a bad thing.

I guess we'll see . . .

Brooke

ROWDY'S JOINT WORKED FOR ALL of twenty minutes, before I was back to torturing myself with thoughts of Jameson.

It's already past three in the morning and all I can manage to do is toss and turn, driving myself crazy with numerous thoughts.

My conversation with Jameson has been running through my head for the last hour though, making me think about my mother and her house now.

I blame Rowdy for making me think even deeper than I already was to begin with.

Sitting up from bed, I reach for the jeans I took off and slip them back on, before jumping up and reaching for my jacket.

It's been almost two years since I've been back to my mother's place.

I think it's time I suck it up and go back.

I need to figure out what work's left to be done and get it taken care of.

For her.

The truth is—I'm lonely here—I hate this apartment. It makes me feel so far away from my mother. I miss the comfort of her house.

Before I can give myself enough time to change my mind, I rush out the door and jump into my car.

When I get to the big, brick house, I park out front and take a few minutes to prepare myself for the emotions of being here again.

I know it's going to overwhelm me. But maybe feeling anything other than what I've been feeling for the last week will be a good thing.

Taking a deep breath, I make my way up the porch steps and dig into my purse for the key.

My jaw drops when I push the door open to see the living room floor is no longer a mess of hardwood flooring, waiting to be finished.

It's done. The whole thing. Not one plank is out of place and it looks amazing.

Stunned, I walk inside and close the door behind me, allowing the tears to flow as I look around the empty room.

"What is going on?" I whisper to myself, overwhelmed with emotions. "Who did this?"

I freeze and my head shoots up, when I hear a noise come from the kitchen.

A part of me is a little creeped out someone is lurking around my mother's abandoned house in the middle of the night, but the bigger part of me is thankful and extremely curious as to who the hell would do this.

With caution, I walk through the living room, noticing a small light on the kitchen floor, once I get close enough to look inside the door.

That's when I notice a dirty Jameson, on his knees, working

on the tile.

"What . . . how . . ." I'm completely speechless as he looks up at me, his eyes softening once he sees my emotional expression.

"I asked Karson for a key last week."

"But she didn't even tell me . . ."

"I asked her not to," he says, while wiping his hands off and standing up. "Wanted it to be a surprise so you could move back, if you chose to."

He watches me carefully, slowly moving closer to me as if he's fighting hard to stay away, but is losing the battle.

Is it bad I want him to give in and lose it?

"Wow . . ." I toss my purse down and move further into the kitchen, taking a look around. "I can't believe you've done all this so quickly. Thank you, Jameson."

I can see his muscles flex, his body becoming rigid, the closer I get to him. "I didn't want you to have to wait too long, when you've already waited long enough. I've been coming here on all of my spare time."

My eyes land on his, my heartbeat quickening from his words. "You didn't have to do that for me. I know you must have other stuff going on."

"I don't," he says quickly. Almost too quickly as if he wants to make that part extra clear. "This is my top priority right now."

"I . . . I don't know what to say, but thank you. This means a lot to me."

"I know," he whispers. "That's why I'm doing it."

As much as I know I should keep a safe distance from Jameson, I find myself jumping into his arms, meaning to give him a quick hug, but his grip on me tightens, pulling me back against him, when I go to pull away.

I can feel our hearts hammering together as Jameson roughly cups my face and moves in even closer, as if our bodies already touching isn't enough for him.

His hard body against mine has me melting into him, wanting more, as his eyes search mine.

"Fuck . . . I can't stop thinking about you, Brooke." His grip on my face tightens as he leans down, until his lips are hovering above mine, not even an inch away. "I've been trying to be good. I've been trying so fucking hard to do the right thing, but seeing you today, made it close to impossible and seeing you now . . . I'm completely screwed."

My breath gets knocked out by his lips crushing mine and before I know it, my legs are wrapped around his waist and he's slamming me against the sink as if he's completely lost any control he has left.

With his lips still capturing mine, he lifts my ass up and above the sink, before setting me down and removing my jacket so he can yank my shirt over my head and throw it across the room.

He's so rough right now, making me want to go crazy and just get lost in him.

My hands move along his tight body with a desperation I haven't felt in a long time, pulling at his shirt and jeans as if I'm some kind of fucking wild animal.

It's a struggle, but I finally manage to get his shirt over his chest and pull it over his head, before moving back down to his pants.

Loud moans escape me as his lips move with perfection against mine, consuming every bit of me.

All that exists in this moment is his mouth on mine and his hands leaving trails of fire along my skin from his heated touch.

I want this. I need this . . . desperately.

Growling into my mouth, he tangles both hands into the back of my hair and pulls as he pushes his hips into me, making me aware of his erection as he grinds it against me. "Shit," he growls against my lips. "I want to take you home with me so fucking bad."

Moving my arms up to wrap around his neck, I pull him down to me so I can bite his bottom lip, wanting nothing more than to taste him. "Then do it, Jameson," I say breathlessly. "I want you to just as bad. You have no idea how crazy I've been over you."

His breathing picks up against my lips as if he's thinking about the possibility.

"Fuuuuck!" His grip on my hair releases, before he backs away from me and grips onto his own hair in frustration. "This should not be happening right now. You're my *best friend's* girl. He might've pulled this shit on me, but I can't . . . I can't fuck him over. No matter how badly I want you."

I sit on the sink, breathing heavily as I watch him pace around the kitchen looking a hot, sweaty mess. My heart aches to still feel him touching me. I hate this. "What do you mean? Cole slept with your girlfriend?"

He stops pacing and reaches to button his jeans back up and throw his shirt back on. "It's complicated, but yes. And in the beginning, making you want me was supposed to be about getting back at him. But now . . ."

I jump off the sink and watch his back muscles flex through his dirty white shirt as he grips the doorframe. "What, Jameson? What about now? Tell me!"

"Now it's about me not hurting my friend when all I really want is to keep you as mine. But . . ." he releases the frame and slowly turns around to face me, his eyes filled with pain. "My want for you is too strong to ignore. This wasn't supposed to happen. I wasn't supposed to *fall* for you, but I did. That's why I need to stay away from you."

My heart stops from his confession.

Everything inside of me is screaming to jump into his arms and never let go, but I can't let him get hurt by all this.

Being together the way we want to be, will do nothing but

destroy what he has with Cole. I can *feel* it and it sucks.

"I can't be with Cole," I say softly, while reaching for my shirt and jacket to get dressed. "I may not be able to be with *you*, but I can't be with *him* either, when you're the only thing I can think about."

He says nothing as I grab my purse and walk away on shaky legs.

It's not until I reach the front door, that I hear him stalking up behind me.

I wait for him to say something. Anything . . . but he doesn't. He just angrily grips the doorframe and closes his eyes as I walk away and jump into my car.

Giving them both up is the only thing I can do at this point.

I'll never be able to be with Cole, knowing that in my heart, I truly want Jameson and can't have him.

Tomorrow, I'm letting Cole go. I just hope he doesn't hate Jameson for it . . .

CHAPTER NINETEEN

Brooke

WHEN I TEXTED COLE LAST night to let him know we needed to speak in person, the last thing I expected was for him to show up here, at my work.

My heart about stops the moment I lay eyes on him, walking through the door. The look on his face makes it clear he's worried about what I have to say.

This is *not* the place I wanted to have this conversation, but I know I need to let him go before things get in too deep with us.

The last thing I want to do is lead him on and make him believe I want more from him, when I don't.

I was confused at first. I admit it.

Thought maybe if I went a few days without seeing or talking to Jameson that I'd stop thinking about him and focus back on Cole, but I was wrong.

Seeing Jameson doing work at my mother's house last night, instead of him being with another girl like I expected, only made me want him more and bring to the surface all the feelings I was trying to push away for him.

No one has ever done anything like this for me before and Jameson did it all on his own. He did it because he knew it'd make me happy.

We could barely stay away from each other once our eyes met and the intensity of our heated kiss, made me well aware of the fact that I'm completely falling for Jameson and not even time or space is going to be enough to stop that right now.

I *need* to do this. I *can* do this.

Karson grabs the towel out of my hand and whispers in my ear that she's got it. "Go out back and talk to Cole. I'll be fine."

When I look back up, Cole nervously runs his hand through his messy hair and nods for me to follow him, so I do.

Placing his hand on my lower back, he opens the door for me, guiding me outside and to the side of the building.

My heart feels as if it's about to jump through my ribcage at any moment.

How the hell am I supposed to say this?

I stayed awake all night, tossing and turning, trying to think of the best way to tell Cole that we need to stop seeing each other.

Nothing and I mean *nothing* sounded good enough in my head.

Oh, by the way . . . I can't sleep with you anymore, the sex was great and all, but I've fallen for your best friend who doesn't even want to touch me, because he knows you care about me and will be hurt.

No. Just no.

"Talk to me," Cole whispers, while backing me up against the building and pinning me in with his arms. "I want you to be able to tell me what's on your mind, Brooke. Even if you think it's going to upset me. I'm not blind. I know something's been bothering you all week. I hate you've waited this long to want to talk about it."

I nervously pull my eyes away from his, unable to hold his

intense stare. Hurt already lingers there, making this moment even harder to go forward with. "I can't do whatever it is we're doing, anymore. Everything has become . . ."

"Complicated?" he questions.

"Yes," I say softly. "I'm feeling really confused about my feelings right now and what I should do with them. I don't want anyone to get hurt."

I look up into Cole's eyes when his finger gently lifts my chin toward him. "And those feelings aren't for me, right. That's what you're getting at?"

"I'm sorry," escapes me, before I can think of a better response. "I've never messed around with two guys at the same time before, Cole. I didn't expect any real feelings to form from anyone's part. I've spent the last week, trying to figure mine out and now I have."

"I see." He lets out a frustrated breath and moves his hand along the back of my neck, before gripping it as he moves in closer. "Are you sure you feel *nothing* for me?"

"I . . . I don't know. I mean I do, but . . ."

Before I can finish what I'm about to say, Cole closes the distance between us, kissing me with so much passion that it almost takes my breath away.

But it's not because I feel something deeply for him like I do for Jameson, it's because I wasn't expecting it and it has my head going crazy, thinking I'm doing something wrong.

It's making it hard to breathe.

After a few seconds, I place my hands to Cole's chest and gently push him away, making Cole pull on my bottom lip, before he releases it. "Nothing?" His question is breathy against my lips as he searches my eyes for the answer.

"I'm sorry, Cole. I *do* feel something, but it's not strong enough for me to stop feeling what I feel for Jameson. Doesn't matter though . . ."

"Why? Why the fuck doesn't it matter? Of course it does."

I release a breath and push away from the building, feeling guilty. "Jameson cares about you and hurting your guy's friendship is the last thing I want to do. I'll stay away from him. So, it *doesn't* matter. He plans to do the same too."

I force a smile and kiss him on the cheek so I can end this conversation, before I get too emotional. "I should really get back inside. The rush will be coming soon and Karson is too crazy to handle it on her own. She gets distracted easily."

He closes his eyes, but doesn't bother looking my direction as I begin backing away.

It's not until I almost turn the corner that he speaks again. "Did Jameson tell you he's staying away from you?"

I stop and nod my head. "He made it very clear. Yes."

"Okay," he says gently. "That's all I need to hear."

My heart hurts at the reminder of Jameson pushing me away last night, but I need to focus on work.

My job is the most important thing right now. It's important because I need to save up the extra cash to finish what my mom and Jameson started.

There's no reason Jameson should want to stick around to finish it. There's nothing left to happen between us and he made that clear last night.

So, I'm going to pull my big girl panties on, go back in that door and make this happen.

I'm going to be strong and do my best to forget both these boys all together.

I was a fool to believe this would be easy . . .

NOT EVEN FIVE MINUTES AFTER I walk in the damn door and
pour a drink, I hear Cole's Charger pull into the driveway.

My guess is he's here to chew my ass out for seeing Brooke
last night, when seeing her wasn't even my intention. It happened
by accident.

I was just hoping to get by with finishing up her mother's
house without her finding me. All I want is for her to be happy.
Even if it's not *with* me, I'll get a little peace in knowing some of
her happiness is *because* of me.

"Well . . . fuck. This should be good."

The last thing I feel like dealing with right now is Cole. My
head is still fucked up from last night and I'm on edge.

With my arm resting against the brick, I stare down into the
flames, listening as Cole walks in and pours himself a drink.

It's otherwise quiet in this big house.

"Got a message from Brooke late last night telling me we
needed to talk in person." His voice is tight as he speaks. "Just left
her work after a nice little conversation."

With my arm still resting against the fireplace, I tilt my head
up to look at him as he stands beside me with his eyes focused on
his glass.

"Say what you have to say, Cole. Go ahead. Fucking get it all
out. Let's not drag this out."

My words cause him to clench his jaw and slam his drink back.
"I need another. You good?"

I nod, just wanting him to hurry the fuck up and get this over
with.

"Why the hell are you so sweaty and dirty right now?" he
questions, while looking me over.

"Just got home from working on a little project," I say stiffly. "Let's get to what you really came here to talk about, Cole. All I want is to finish this drink and go to sleep. Your ass is slowing me down."

His arm flexes as he squeezes his glass and takes a quick swig of Jack, before speaking. "I knew something was off with Brooke this whole week. I fucking felt her distancing herself from me. Come to find out, there's a damn good reason for that."

I stiffly take a drink, waiting for him to continue.

"She fell for my best fucking friend," he growls. "And as much as I want to kill your ass for it, she made it clear you plan to leave her alone. Is that true?"

I pull my eyes away from the flames, to turn around and face him. "Yeah. I'm not a complete asshole. We've been friends for almost our entire damn lives." I release a frustrated breath and tilt back my glass. "You have my word that I'll stay away from Brooke."

"Good." He slams his empty glass down and locks eyes with me. "I'd hate to lose our friendship over a woman. And like you said before, it's always over a girl. Especially when that girl is mine." He points at me. "So, stay away from her. What she needs is a little time to remember what we had *before* you came into the picture. Maybe some time away from you will allow her to clear her head and think straight."

"You have my word," I say through clenched teeth. I'm so close to losing my shit on him. I hope like hell he's about done with this conversation.

Brooke doesn't want him.

Maybe a little time will clear his fucking head to that.

"Thanks, man." He slaps my shoulder and then squeezes it. "I know you didn't plan for shit to happen this way. So, I respect you backing off even though it's clear you have feelings for her too. After all, she was mine first."

Just like Katie was mine.

But hell, I'm not bringing that up. To tell the truth, I'm glad he got rid of her for me. He was right, she did have me blinded to her disloyalty to me.

He did me a favor and now, I'm doing him one by backing off and respecting his feelings for Brooke.

I'm already hating myself for it. Guess that makes me a shitty friend.

"Yeah . . ."

Cole's grip on my shoulder releases. "You're a good friend, man."

With that, he walks away.

I wait until I hear the door close behind him, before I growl out and chuck my glass at the fireplace, watching as the glass shatters against the brick.

Anger courses through me as I reach for a cigarette and light it, before grabbing the rest of the bottle of Jack and making my way upstairs.

Let's just hope I still have a spare bottle hidden in my room, because I'm gonna need it to drown out this pain.

Staying away from Brooke is going to be one of the hardest things I've ever had to do. *Forgetting her will be even harder . . .*

CHAPTER TWENTY

One Week Later . . .

Brooke

'VE SPENT THIS LAST WEEK losing myself in work, being sure to pick up every available shift at *BJ's Place* I can get.

It's the only thing that's been able to distract me just enough to keep my mind from wandering to Jameson and how much it hurts, now that I know for *sure* he won't be coming around anymore.

It hasn't been enough to completely take my mind off him, but I didn't expect it to. I don't expect anything to at this point. I'm just hoping that with time, the memories of the way his touch and kiss made me feel, will begin to fade and eventually he'll just get out of my head and stop torturing me.

A week has done little so far.

My mind is seriously driving me insane. It's as if I've lost all control over it, because as soon as it gets a quiet moment to think, it goes *back* to Jameson.

And trust me, the fact Cole has been sending me random texts to check on me, hasn't made it any easier to forget *his* friend. The one *he* brought into my life. It's because of Cole I fell for Jameson to begin with.

All because he pushed Jameson into a reason to get back at him and now we're all screwed.

Needing to get some air and just breathe, I hop out of bed and slip my jacket on.

It's a nice night and my mother's house is only about a fifteen-minute walk from here.

I've been meaning to snap a few pictures of the unfinished kitchen to send to some guy Ben knows. Said he'd be able to get me a discount and the guy's a fast and highly skilled worker.

Ever since I caught Jameson working on the floor last week, I've been kicking my own ass for not having it done a long time ago. I guess I just wasn't ready to live there again and I wasn't ready to admit that was the real reason I never had someone come in and finish it.

But walking into the house to see the living room complete, had me wanting to move back in like crazy. I've missed being there so much and Jameson was able to remind me of that.

I owe him so much for that.

I find myself smiling, the moment the house comes into view. It has me walking faster, wanting to get inside and take another look at the beautiful job Jameson did in the living room.

Since I know I won't be getting much sleep tonight, sticking around and setting up the furniture sounds like the best plan. It'll be the first step to making this place feel like home again.

Excitement courses through me as I rush up the steps and unlock the door, pushing it open.

I'm completely unprepared for what I see next.

"Oh my god." I throw my hand over my mouth in shock and

walk inside, my eyes taking in the already furnished room.

Everything is set up already.

Did Jameson do this?

Karson hasn't mentioned Jameson or the fact he might still have her key, but I know there's no way Karson has had any time to surprise me with this. She values her sleep more than anyone I know. So, when she's not working or hanging out with me, she's getting her beauty sleep.

Emotions overwhelm me as I step inside and close the door behind me. It's been a while since I've felt at home anywhere, but I feel more at home than ever right now.

"I can't believe this . . ."

I walk past the couch, running my hand over the gray fabric with a smile. My mother was so excited when she purchased this thing, along with the fancy decorative pillows. She barely let me sit on it for the first week.

Said it was the first nice thing she'd been able to buy for herself in a long time and wanted time to enjoy it before me or Karson spilled anything on it.

I was nineteen then. Two years before my mother passed and now it's been two years since. It's crazy how the time flies.

After taking a few minutes to enjoy the sight of seeing this place look like a home again, I make my way to the kitchen, surprised to see the floor in here is done as well.

"Jameson finished it," I whisper in wonder. "I can't believe . . ."

My heart aches for Jameson even more now than ever.

He still took the time to finish my mother's house, even though he knew we'd be staying away from each other.

I don't know one other guy so selfless that he'd be willing to do something like this for someone else. Especially one he's not even dating or sleeping with.

He had no reason to continue coming around to finish the

job, yet he did with no questions asked.

With my hands shaking, I reach into my pocket and pull my phone out, scrolling down to Jameson's last text message.

Jameson: But like I said . . . I'm a little more generous. Tell me where you live.

I read over his message a few times, feeling my heart go crazy inside my chest at the memory of that night.

It was one of the most exciting things to happen to me. The way he just showed up at my apartment and took charge, giving me a show, with the confidence he'd be able to make me come without even touching me.

And he was right.

That was the moment I knew I needed to feel him inside of me. I knew I needed him and I still do.

Exhaling, I stare down at my phone, trying to decide if it's best to wait a while before thanking him. It might be too soon to talk to him after what happened here last week.

I need time to forget how damn good it felt.

I run my hand through my hair in frustration, while taking a seat on the couch and tossing my phone down beside me.

Getting comfortable, I lay back and stare up at the ceiling, thinking of old times with my mom and how easy it was to talk to her. I miss her so much right now. What I wouldn't give to be able to ask her advice.

Do I listen to my heart and go after Jameson? Or do I listen to my head and do what's best for him and Cole?

I've never been so confused in my entire life.

An hour must pass, of me driving myself crazy, before I reach for my phone to see it's just past three in the morning.

I didn't plan on sleeping here tonight, because I didn't expect the house to be ready for me to move back into, but now that I'm here, I don't want to leave.

Jumping up from the couch, I walk over to lock the front door, but freeze when I hear what sounds like a motorcycle, pulling into the driveway.

I can barely breathe when I open the door to see Jameson pulling his helmet off and jumping off his bike.

He doesn't notice me standing here at first, but becomes motionless when he looks my direction, our eyes meeting for the first time in a week.

Holy beautiful man, I think I'm going to die here on the spot.

It's hard not to notice how dangerously sexy he looks, standing there all tense in a black leather jacket and ripped up jeans, his jaw muscles flexing as he looks me over.

His face is covered in a thick stubble that only makes him look that much more dangerous and sexy right now.

I can hardly stand to look at him without wanting to jump into his arms and crush my lips against his.

"Jameson . . . hi."

Keep your cool, Brooke. You can do this . . .

Jameson

THE LAST THING I WAS prepared for tonight was setting my eyes on Brooke.

I came back tonight with the intent of making sure everything in the house is in working order, before giving Karson back her key and telling her to let Brooke know the house is move in ready.

Seeing Brooke has my alpha side going crazy, making me want

to throw her over my shoulder and claim her as mine.

Has me thinking, *fuck Cole. If he puts his hands on her again, I'll rip his heart out and feed it to him. I want to be the only one touching and kissing her for now on.*

Well doesn't this just make me a huge asshole . . .

"I wasn't expecting you to be here."

"I was thinking the same," she replies with a small smirk. "Thank you for *everything* you did for me. Means more than you know."

I can't pull my eyes away from her as she steps outside and closes the door behind her. Everything inside of me is going crazy to have her near me and I think I have a way of making that happen that doesn't involve me throwing her around the house and kissing her like I really want to.

My eyes lock with her as I hold out my helmet. "Come with me."

She looks confused, but makes her way down the steps and reaches for my helmet, without question.

My eyes close and my heart hammers against my chest, when I feel her climb onto the bike behind me, and wrap her arms around my waist.

"Just like last time. Let me . . ."

"I like it when you go fast," she says quickly. "I trust you."

Hearing Brooke say she trusts me, fucks with my head, causing me to steel my jaw and cuss to myself.

Truthfully, I don't trust myself with her and I know if I allow myself to stay with her for too long, that I'll give in and fuck up my friendship with Cole.

But leaving her right now, when I've only just got her in my sight again after a torturous week without her, is not an option for me.

I take off before I can talk myself out of it, feeling her arms tighten around me, as she leans into my back, burying her face into my leather jacket.

It feels so fucking good having her close to me.

We ride for a good thirty minutes, neither one of us finding a reason to want to stop and end this night yet.

I have no idea when I'll get this opportunity again, so I just keep on riding, giving her the chance to turn us back around when she's ready.

She must be thinking the same thing as me, because another thirty or so minutes goes by and I still feel her holding onto me as if she's not ready to let go yet.

"Fuck," I mutter to myself, when we pass the spot we first kissed at.

She must notice it too, because her grip on me tightens and she lifts her head over my shoulder to get a good look.

That's when I know it's time to take her back.

Because my urge to kiss her and put my hands all over her body is stronger now, making me want to stop my bike and take her right here.

A man can only handle so much before he gives in and takes what he wants, and I haven't wanted anything but Brooke since the moment I laid eyes on her.

I reach behind me and scoot Brooke's ass forward, letting her know she needs to hold on tight, before I speed up.

Her hands grab at me, moving slightly up my body as if she's turned on right now and is fighting with everything in her not to touch me like she wants to.

Even with concentrating on the road, I can feel her heart hammering against my back as her fingertips dig into the ridges of my muscles.

Fuck, I need to get her home and now.

When we pull up in front of the brick house, I grab her hand

and help her off the back of my bike, fighting like hell to stay on my bike and not go inside.

"I'll come back sometime this week and take a look at things to make sure the house doesn't need maintenance work done. I want to make sure you don't have any issues."

She smiles and hands me my helmet. "You're incredible for doing this for me. Thank you, Jameson." Without hesitation, she grabs my face and presses her lips against my cheek.

My free hand instantly reaches out to grab the back of her head, holding her still, as I brush my lips against hers, before speaking against them. "It's taking everything I have right now not to kiss you, Brooke. Go inside and lock the door."

I can feel her breath against my lips, her breathing picking up as my teeth graze her bottom lip. "What if I don't want to keep you out?"

"Then I won't be able to stop myself from giving you what I know you deserve, but I can't give." I brush my thumb over her cheek. "I won't be strong enough to stop myself from making you mine."

"Then . . ." she backs away from me, keeping her eyes on me the whole time. "I'll keep the door unlocked. Because I'm just as weak as you are."

My hands shake as I grip the handlebars, fighting like hell to keep control, as she disappears into the house.

It only takes two seconds, before I hop off my bike and toss my helmet down, realizing this is a battle I won't win.

I want Brooke and not even my friendship with Cole is enough to stop me from taking her . . .

CHAPTER TWENTY-ONE

Jameson

RUSHING UP THE STEPS, I push the door open, my heart racing as my eyes land on Brooke.

She's standing by the couch, looking just as sexually frustrated as I am, her chest quickly rising and falling as she watches me close the door behind me and step inside.

"Fuck this shit," I growl out. "You're *mine*."

Stalking toward her, I grip the back of her hair, and slam my lips against hers, kissing her hard, as she jumps into my arms and wraps her legs around my waist.

She instantly grabs onto my hair, her fingers twisting and pulling on it, as she moans into my mouth, getting lost in our kiss.

The taste of her mouth has me losing control, biting her bottom lip a little too hard, before I run my tongue over it and pull it into my mouth to soothe it.

I've been desperate for days to feel her mouth on mine again and now that I am, I can't get enough of it.

I *need* her taste on me. I want to *feel* her all around me as I make her come.

Feeling like an untamed beast, I slam her against the wall and rip the front of her shirt open, before lifting her up to take her hard nipple in my mouth.

This has Brooke digging her nails into my back and pulling at my shirt, trying to take it off me.

"I need this off, Jameson. Now."

Holding her up with my body, I lift my arms, allowing her to yank my shirt over my head and toss it aside, before I grab her again. The sound that leaves her mouth as she looks down at me has my cock straining to break free from my jeans.

"And I need *everything* off." I grip her throat and gently squeeze it, while leaning in to speak against her ear. "Your pussy is mine, Brooke. One *taste* and I became addicted. *Nothing* will be able to keep me away from you after this. Not even Cole."

I feel her swallow, before she speaks. "Good. I don't want you away from me, Jameson. I can't handle it anymore. I *need* you."

Pure, raw need has me dropping her to her feet and yanking her jeans and panties down her legs, before yanking at my own zipper and pulling out my hard cock.

With one hand gripping the back of her neck, I lift her thigh with the other and thrust into her, causing her to moan out in a mixture of pain and pleasure as I fill her pussy.

"Holy fuck!" I groan into her neck. "You're so wet for me, baby. I love it."

Breathing heavily, I press my forehead against hers, making eye contact, as I pull out of her and quickly push back in.

"Jameson . . ." She closes her eyes, leaning her head into mine, as she fights to even her breathing. "I've wanted *this* since the night you came to my apartment."

"What's that? Tell me . . ."

She opens her eyes, when I gently brush my mouth across hers. "For you to take me, *alone.*"

Her words have me pulling out and pushing back in as deeply as I can, wanting her to feel me deeper than Cole has ever been.

I feel her body shudder in my arms as I slowly move in and out of her, gripping her thigh tightly to keep her from falling over.

Being inside her bare, feels even better than I imagined. The idea that I'd never get to feel her this way had me losing my shit.

I'm just hoping like hell Cole has never been inside her like this. There's no way I'd be able to look at him without wanting to kill him.

Our sweaty bodies, move together, our hearts racing as we get lost in each other and in this moment.

As much as I'd love to take it easy on her and show her how much I really care for her, my need to take her deep and hard is taking over, causing my rhythm to speed up as I slam into her.

Within seconds, I have Brooke screaming my name, clawing at my sweaty back as I shove her up the wall with each hard thrust.

The sound of our wet bodies slapping together has me wanting to come inside of her right now, but I'm not even close to being done with her.

When we're through, I don't want her thinking about any other guy. I want to fuck the memory of me and Cole taking her at the same time out of her fucking mind.

Me being rough with her must turn her on even more, because before I know it, Brooke's other leg is wrapping around my waist and she's bouncing up and down on my dick as if to show me she owns it.

Apparently, I'm not the only one wanting to make something clear here tonight.

With one arm wrapped around the back of her neck and my other hand gripping at her hips, I back away from the wall, holding her tightly as she continues to ride me.

Her loud moans fill my ear, getting me so fucking heated that I begin pulling her body down on top of mine, my hips roughly thrusting her back up each time she comes down.

"Jameson!" She screams next to my ear and squeezes my neck with her arms, holding onto me to for dear life. "Don't stop! Don't ever fucking stop. Please . . ."

Holding onto her, I bury my face into her neck, before running my tongue up it, tasting the sweat that was put there by me.

This has her moaning even louder and grinding her hips into me as if she's completely lost it now.

"Fuck me . . ." I walk into the kitchen and set her down in front of the kitchen island, turning her around to face it. Luckily for this next position, it doesn't stand very tall.

Coming up behind her, I run my hand over her right thigh, before lifting it up high and holding it, while she rests her elbow on the marble counter for support.

I gently bite her neck as I slide into her from behind, stopping once I'm in as deep as I can go. This position makes her even tighter than she already was, so I have to be careful I don't come too fast.

I want her to come first. She'll always get pleasure before I do. That's how it works with me.

She throws her head back and bites her bottom lip, moaning out as I begin moving inside her, starting out slow at first, before I speed up, taking her hard.

"Oh shit, Jameson. You feel so good." She repositions herself so she's leaning over the counter, gripping onto the edge as I pound into her, going harder as faster with each thrust. "I'm about to . . ."

She cries out her release, her body shaking as her pussy clenches around my dick.

I give her body a minute to come down from its high, before I pull out of her and pick her up, setting her down on the kitchen island.

Running my hands up her thighs, I move in between her legs and press my lips against hers, as I slowly ease my way back inside her, kissing her through her sensitive moans.

"Bite me if you have to."

I grip her hips with both hands and thrust in fast and hard, causing her to bite into my shoulder and scream as I take her.

"Can I come inside you?" I ask against her ear.

She nods and digs her nails into my back. "I'm on the pill."

Her approval has me slamming into her a few more times, before I bury myself as deep as I can go and come inside her. We both moan into each other's mouth, her coming undone at the same time.

I swear I could stay like this all night with her.

Our naked bodies plastered together. Us breathing against each other as we come down from our high.

This moment feels so fucking real.

Brooke is meant for me. I know this more now than ever.

Cole will have no choice but to accept that.

I'm making her mine . . .

Brooke

HOLY SHIT. I CAN'T BREATHE.

How the hell am I supposed to breathe when Jameson just took me, bare, and came inside me.

I've never felt anything so passionate in my life. Not even both boys taking me at the same time had me fighting for air, the way I am at this very moment, here in Jameson's arms.

His body against mine, his strong arms holding me tight, is

the best thing in the world to me right now.

I never want this moment to end.

"You okay?" Jameson kisses the side of my neck, before working his way back up to my mouth. "Relax and breathe . . ."

I close my eyes and work on steadying my breathing, but the moment his lips meet mine, it becomes hard to breathe again.

This man is going to be the death of me.

"How am I supposed to breathe with your sexy lips on mine?" I smile against his mouth and run my hands through his sweaty hair. "Or this sexy body?"

He growls against my lips, before kissing me hard and deep. "I'm wondering the same thing." He smiles as I slap his chest. "I meant your sexy lips and body. Not mine."

I shake my head and bite his lip, causing his grip on the back of my head to tighten. "Mmm . . . bite me again and I won't give you a chance to breathe. Biting turns me on, baby."

His body towers over mine, plastering me against the countertop as he kisses my neck. It has my heart going crazy and my stomach filling with butterflies.

I jump when his teeth nip my neck, totally not expecting it at this moment. "Ouch!"

He laughs against my neck and then stands up, pulling me up to sit up straight. "I'll look for some blankets so we can make a bed in the living room for tonight. We'll get your bedroom set up this week."

I find myself smiling like a silly little girl. "You're spending the night?"

He nods his head and then pulls me in for a kiss. "Of course I am. There's no way I'm allowing you to feel lonely, your first night back in the house. I'm not going anywhere."

Happiness swarms through me, making my insides warm and cozy at the thought of Jameson and I spending the night together.

This is real. This moment is really happening.

I know I should feel somewhat guilty, but I just can't. Not right now.

All I want is to wrap myself up in Jameson's arms and feel his heart beating against me as I fall asleep.

And that's exactly what is happening.

Twenty minutes later, Jameson has the floor all set up with a huge pile of soft, fluffy blankets, and he's pulling me down into his arms, holding me against him.

He's holding me tight as if he doesn't want to let go.

This moment is perfect and I know for a fact it wouldn't feel this way with anyone else but Jameson . . .

CHAPTER TWENTY-TWO

Jameson

WAKING UP WITH BROOKE IN my arms was one of the best feelings I've had in a long time.

Not to mention I slept like a fucking baby last night. I can't even remember the last time I've slept through the whole night, without waking up and thinking for hours, allowing stress to overwhelm me.

Having her wrapped in my arms makes me feel at peace. It seems to keep all the negative bullshit out of my head and allows me to feel happy for once.

She's special to me and I plan to make sure Cole knows that. He might hate me for a while or even for good, but I can't turn my back on Brooke.

I tried and it didn't work. I won't attempt it again. Even if it means losing Cole's friendship.

Leaving her alone was the hardest shit I ever had to do. It killed me and ate at me, making it impossible.

I smile as Brooke comes out of my bathroom, still dressed in the t-shirt I gave her this morning when we came to my house.

I wanted the chance to spend the day with her, to just relax in bed and watch whatever TV shows or movies she's into.

Doesn't matter to me just as long as she's in *my* bed and in *my* arms.

My house seemed like the best place to go so I could show her just how welcome she is in my home.

I want her to be able to show up at any time and know she's free to do whatever she wants here.

She's my woman and she'll always get anything and everything she wants. Her needs will come first.

"Come here . . ." I pull her back into bed with me and roll over on top of her, pulling the sheet over our heads.

Her laughter fills the sheet, causing me to smile against her lips before I kiss her. "This might just end up being the third time today we've had sex. I'm not sure you can handle anymore of me."

"Is that right?" She nips my lip, before tugging on it with her teeth. "I think it would be the fourth, actually. You're horrible at counting."

"Maybe I wasn't keeping count," I say against her lips. "Everything's a blur when it comes to having you in my arms. I can barely remember my own fucking name from seeing you naked. Fuck. . . . Brooke. You have me losing my mind."

"I like hearing that . . ." She runs her hands down my chest, before lowering them down my abs and then my dick.

Without hesitation, she spreads her legs and guides it to her pussy, allowing me to slowly enter her.

"Mmmm . . ." she moans, with her mouth pressed against my bicep. "I could stay here all day with you."

I hold the sheet over our heads with one hand, while gently grabbing her head with the other as I begin moving inside her.

Even after all the times we've had sex since last night, it still amazes me at how good it feels to be inside her.

I know she's sore by now, so I'm gentle this time, being sure not to hurt her as I slowly grind my hips between her thighs.

The feel of her bare pussy, hugging my dick has my insides going crazy. I still can't believe I'm inside her this way.

It's not long, before I feel her clench down around me as she shakes below me from her orgasm.

I follow not long after, pushing in deep and letting go inside her *again*.

After finding out no other man has been inside her this way, I don't think I'll be able to have sex with her and *not* want to fill her with my come.

Brooke is mine in every fucking way.

She kisses me and rolls us over, running her fingers over my chest as she straddles me. "Looks like we'll have to shower, *again*."

"We will . . ." I pull her face down and kiss all over it, making her smile. "When we feel like it. I don't have anywhere to be for another three hours. Just relax and let me cater to you."

Grinning, she hops off me and rushes to the bathroom to most likely clean up a bit. She comes back a few minutes later and crawls back into my arms, relaxing as I rub her body.

We've spent most of the day talking about our lives, filling each other in on everything we feel like the other should know.

I'm not trying to rush all that stuff. The point of being with someone is getting to know all the little details along the way.

I know all the things I need to know about her at the moment. I've known just enough all along to know I wanted her in my life.

Right now, I just want to lay here in silence and take care of Brooke until I have to leave for the club tonight.

I want to enjoy this moment with her until I have to break the news to Cole and possibly take a few hits.

Hell, he might even kill my ass for this, but Brooke is worth it . . .

EVEN THOUGH BROOKE OFFERED TO be there when I tell Cole about the two of us, I want her as far away as possible in case he loses his shit and explodes.

She doesn't need to see that.

I'm the man. I'll take the heat for this.

I'm the one that couldn't stay away from her even after Cole asked me to. I'm the one that barged into the house and decided to slam her against the wall and make her mine.

Therefore, I'll be the one to take Cole's anger. It's nothing I haven't dealt with before in the twenty years I've known his ass.

Leaning against the wall, I look around at the five poker tables, making sure none of these assholes look as if they're about to try to run or some shit.

Rev went on his break fifteen minutes ago, so as soon as he comes back down, I'm out of this hot ass room and back upstairs with Cole.

Telling him here seems like shitty timing, but it's the only way I'll be able to get it out so I can go home to Brooke, without it being behind my best friend's back. This can't wait any longer.

Plus, it'll keep us from ripping each other's throats out . . . maybe.

I push away from the wall and walk around table number two, when I notice James do a quick look around the room as if he's looking for me.

Sneaky little dick.

Do I really need to make my presence clear with this asshole? I think he truly enjoys me kicking his ass.

"Stay in your seat, James," I say, while roughly pushing his shoulder down as he attempts to stand.

"I was just going to the bathroom. Can't a guy take a piss?"

I shake my head and back away, when I notice Rev enter the room. "No. Hold it."

"Keep your eye on James. Make sure if he gets up that it's only to go to the bathroom. Hold his fucking dick for him if you have to. Maybe that'll get the picture across."

Rev laughs, while putting his earpiece back on. "He's not going anywhere. Right, James?"

"Right," James answers pathetically. "Not unless I want to get my ass kicked."

"Good, boy," Rev says with a smile. "See. I've been on his ass all night."

"Alright, man." I laugh and slap his back. "Call me if you need me to chase anyone down. I'm feeling like a little jog on this beautiful fucking night."

"Will do."

My eyes shoot over in James' direction to see him rolling his eyes and mumbling something under his breath as he tosses down a card. He looks up at me, but quickly turns away when I flex my jaw in annoyance.

That's right, asshole. I'm not in the mood tonight.

I point in James' direction as I back up toward the door. "Try something tonight and I *will* break a hand or two this time. So unless you can play cards with your dick, I suggest you don't leave this room. Got it?"

James' eyes go wide and he quickly turns to Rev. "Is he allowed to do that?"

Rev just smiles and shrugs.

I turn and exit the room.

I feel my blood boiling with each step I take up the stairs, getting closer to the main floor and closer to Cole.

We haven't spoken much tonight, but soon the crowd will start thinning out and we'll have more free time to have our little chat.

It's already slowed down enough up here that only one of us is really needed, so I make my way over to the bar and order a Jack and coke from Violet.

"You look tense. Sure you don't need a shot to go along with this?" She sets the drink down in front of me and watches as I tilt it back. "I'll be happy to pour you one or two."

I shake my head. "Nah, I had Jayla make me about three of these on my break. This is fine."

Violet smiles and eyes me over, seeming to lean in closer and closer, until she's close enough to almost brush her lips against mine. "Have any plans tonight? I'm free and was hoping . . ."

I place my empty glass down and back away, not wanting her to get the impression I want her lips this close to mine. The only lips I want to taste are Brooke's. "I'm taken, V."

"Oh." She looks shocked and disappointed as she reaches for the empty glass. "I thought you and Katie were done?"

"We are." I look over to see Cole watching me from across the room, looking just as tense as I feel. "I fell for someone I wasn't supposed to fall for."

With that, I walk away, my muscles tensing the closer I get to Cole. It's not just because of the fact I have to tell Cole about us, it's the fact that every time I look at his face, I'll be reminded he's been inside Brooke.

That her naked, sweaty body has been pressed against his, Cole making her come for him, probably more times than I have.

Now that shit stings. I hate the thought of anyone else pleasuring her in that way.

Trying to keep my shit together the best I can right now, I step up beside Cole, causing him to pull his eyes away from some asshole, he's been keeping in check. "This dude is about two seconds away from having the pleasure of my foot up his ass." He crosses his arms and turns to face me. "Where the hell have you been? Rev got back from break almost ten minutes ago."

I release a slow breath and run my hand through my hair, trying to think of the best way to lay this shit on him. There's no easy way to tell him I'm making Brooke mine and we hooked up last night and numerous times today.

I'm a huge asshole for what I'm about to say.

"We need to talk about Brooke and this is not going to go well." I watch as he stiffens, the muscles in his arms tightening. "I tried staying away from Brooke, but fuck me, I can't do it anymore. I can't. Not being with her was eating me alive and fucking with my head. Trust me, the last thing I wanted to do was fuck up our friendship and stab you in the back, but . . ."

He shakes his head, his hard eyes coming up to meet mine. "But you did, right? Is that what you're about to fucking tell me, Jameson?"

"I thought I could do this shit and not let my heart get in the way, but I fell for her, man. I went and fucking fell for her like an asshole. I've spent the last two weeks trying to push her from my head and I couldn't. You can hate me all you want, but I'm not backing down from her."

"Then you didn't fucking try hard enough, asshole," he growls, getting in my face. "Tell me this. Did you fuck her? You better help like hell your answer is no. I swear to god . . ." He stops and runs his hands down his face, growling out his frustration. "Just . . . did you?"

I stand straight and look him in the eyes when I say it. He may take a swing at me for it, but I'm not backing down. I'll take what I deserve. I'll be the first to admit it's my fault he's not with the girl he cares about. It's my fault she wants me and not him. And it's also my fault I want her too. "Yeah . . ."

His breathing picks up as he turns around and grips the wall, before punching it, repeatedly. "Fuuuuck! I should kill you right now."

"And I probably deserve it," I admit. "But to be fair. *You* started this shit."

"How many times?" he asks from his place in front of the wall.

I shake my head and release a frustrated breath. He doesn't want to know the answer to that. "Don't ask me that shit. Doesn't matter."

He pushes away from the wall and walks back over to stand in front of me. "It matters to me." He roughly points to his chest. "It matters because you knew I cared about her. I have for a while now and you went after her anyways. So fucking tell me."

"Once last night," I answer stiffly. "And a few times today."

My answer has him swinging out, his fist connecting hard with my jaw.

My muscles flex as the pain shoots through my face, but I stand tall and take it like a man. He deserves to get one punch on me.

His face is livid with anger as he looks me over and moves in close as if he's ready to take another swing.

"I expected that punch. I deserve it so I'll take it. But don't expect me not to swing back if you try that shit again."

"Fuck you."

With that, he swings out again, his fist connecting with my mouth this time.

Fire burns throughout my body, pure rage taking over as I elbow him in the face and then tackle him to the ground, wrapping my hand around his throat.

He swings at me, getting one more hit to my jaw, before my fist pounds repeatedly into his face, his blood covering my knuckles.

We only manage to get a few more hits on each other, before Rowdy is dragging me away from Cole, pulling me into a table we end up knocking over in the process.

"Grab Cole!" Rowdy shouts across the room to Rev.

Cole throws his arms up, pushing Rev away as he attempts to grab him. "Get the fuck off me. Don't touch me, Rev."

I shake my arm, causing Rowdy's grip on me to loosen. My fight isn't with him, it's with Cole, so I'm careful not to take my anger out on him.

After this, Rowdy might be the only friend left I can trust.

My muscles flex as I stand back and keep a close eye on Cole, as he begins pacing and gripping at his hair. I'm not sure he's done yet, but I won't come at him unless he comes back at me first.

"I can't believe this shit!" he yells out before flipping one of the tables over and wiping his hand over his bloody mouth. "Fuck. I should kill him."

"In my office now."

Me and Cole look at each other when Mason's angry voice comes through the earpiece.

Cole is the first one to take off, knocking a beer bottle off a table, before making his way through the crowd that is now standing around, watching us.

"Keep your cool, man," Rowdy says, while squeezing my shoulder. "I knew this shit would happen. You both threw some punches and now it's over. Let's keep it that way."

Feeling tense as hell, I make my way upstairs to Mason's office, ready to take my ass chewing. Hell, it can't be any worse than taking a few blows to the face by your best friend.

Mason looks up, his hard eyes landing on me, when I step into his office. "You both look like shit. What the hell am I supposed to do with this."

I take a seat in the chair next to Cole and hope like hell Mason doesn't fire us both for the little shit show we just put on.

"You do know what your job here is, right?"

"Yeah." I look up to make eye contact with Mason. I've never seen him look so pissed off in all the years I've worked here. "And we're both damn good at it. This shit won't happen again. You have my word."

Mason looks to Cole. "What about yours? Give it to me now or you can walk out that door and never come back."

Cole nods, but doesn't speak.

"Okay good. Here's what's going to happen." He sits up straight in his chair, making sure we're both paying attention. "You will take turns working the front door, until I feel like you can handle being in the same room together. I don't give a shit if it's a week, a month or even a fucking year. I will not have my security team fighting *each other* in my club. Am I clear?"

"Got it." Cole stands and walks around to grip the back of the chair. "Am I good to go now?"

"Not until you, assholes, clean up the mess you made. There's two broken tables and glass all over the floor. You *both* can leave for the night after that."

Once we get downstairs, we both stop to check out the mess we made.

"Well, this is new," I say with an amused laugh, while sweeping up glass like an asshole.

"Never thought we'd be the bitches told to clean up our own mess." Cole grabs the table he flipped over and begins dragging it to the back. "Guess that's what happens when we fall for the same fucking girl."

I feel like shit as I watch Cole leave the room with his face all bloody and swollen from my doing. I'm sure I look just as bad as he does. Hell, I feel it.

This is not how I wanted this to go down tonight. Us beating the shit out of each other in front of the whole club.

Time is the only thing that's going to be able to fix this mess now, because I'm not leaving Brooke alone and he's not going to stop caring about her anytime soon.

How much time is the fucking question . . .

CHAPTER
TWENTY-THREE

Brooke

SLOWLY BLINK MY EYES open when I feel a hard body crawl into bed with me, pinning my body down to the mattress.

My body fills with warmness at the realization that Jameson is back to see me.

When he left for the club, I had no idea what to expect after his talk with Cole. To be honest, a part of me was worried he'd never want to see me again. I was afraid after talking with Cole he'd believe he made a mistake by falling for me.

I was terrified he'd walk away.

Relief washes over me when I feel his lips against my jawline, working their way over toward my mouth. He's so soft and caring right now, that it has my heart melting with each kiss.

"Jameson," I whisper into his neck, while closing my eyes as the masculine smell of his skin surrounds me. "I wasn't sure I'd see you tonight."

"Like I told you . . ." he cups my face with both hands and

kisses my lips, but something feels different. His mouth feels swollen against mine. "Nothing is keeping me away from you."

I open my eyes and grab his face, holding it still so I can attempt to get a good look at it in the darkness.

That's when I see his face is bloodied and bruised, his mouth swollen.

"Oh my God! What happened, Jameson? Are you okay?" I run my hands over his face as panic surges through me. Seeing him this way breaks my heart more than I could have ever imagined. Every single part of me screams and aches to take care of him and take away his pain. "Did Cole do this? You guys fought. I should've been there. I should talk to him too."

"I'm okay." He smiles and pulls my hands away from his face, looking down at me with soft eyes. The way his eyes search mine has my heart beating wild with emotions. "We just got into a little scuffle. Trust me, you didn't want to be there to see it. *I* didn't want you there to see it. I know Cole. He will come to you once he has time to think it over. He needs to cool down first."

Guilt washes over me, making me feel like it's my fault this happened. If I wouldn't have given into my feelings for Jameson, then he wouldn't be fighting with Cole. They'd still be friends and they'd both still be happy.

"I'm sorry," I whisper, while shaking my head and removing his hands from my face. "I didn't want this. I don't want you and Cole to hate each other over me. It's not right."

I'm so overwhelmed with emotions I can't stop the tears from falling down my face. Seeing Jameson hurt is killing me so much.

He pulls me into his arms, holding me against him as tightly as possible, while kissing my neck and whispering for me not to cry.

"Shhh . . ." he whispers just below my ear, sending chills up and down my body. "I never want to see your tears. I'll always want to kill whoever is the cause of them. Even if that person is me."

He rolls us over, maneuvering his body to lay between my legs. Having him there makes it so hard not to want to run my hands all over every inch of muscle.

I feel him smile against my lips, right before he pulls the sheet over our heads and begins kissing all over my face, while pressing his body harder against mine.

After a few more kisses, he surprises me by using his teeth.

A laugh immediately escapes me, this moment reminding me of how playful he was with me last night.

I find it to be amazing just how easy it is for Jameson to make me forget about everything else around us and just focus on him.

On his body against mine. His lips caressing my face. The feel of his breath against my skin as he lays on top of me.

He is all that matters in this moment and I want nothing more than to continue feeling this way.

Jameson Daniels . . . is everything I could ever hope for.

I just hope I can be the same for him . . .

IT'S BEEN FIVE DAYS NOW since Jameson told Cole about us and it's been eating at me that I haven't had a chance to talk to Cole yet.

I don't feel right just leaving things how they are right now. I *care* about Cole and I care about his and Jameson's friendship. He's a good guy, he just wasn't the *right* guy. Hurting him wasn't my intention and I hate it had to happen.

I'm just about to leave work for the night and I know for a fact Cole will be working the front door at the club. I know this because Jameson said he'd be working in section A and they're still not allowed to work together yet.

With it being a Tuesday, I'm hoping it'll be slow enough that

I'll get a chance to pull him away for a few seconds and apologize for getting in between him and Jameson.

My heart beats harder and faster, the closer I get to the club, my nerves really starting to take over.

"You can do this. Just say what you need to say and leave."

I pull up at the club and easily find a parking space. Just as expected, they're slow and no one is waiting outside to get in.

I can't tell from where I'm at who's working the door, but it doesn't look to be Cole or Jameson.

Taking a deep breath, I undo my seatbelt and push the door open. As soon as I step out of my car, my eyes land on Cole walking from across the parking lot toward his Charger.

He stops walking and looks my direction, once he notices me parked just a little more than a few spots over. The first thing I notice when he looks at me is his face is just as beat up and bruised as Jameson's. Maybe even worse.

"Leaving for the night?" I question with my heart racing.

He nods his head. "Yeah." His eyes look me over for a few seconds, before he begins walking toward me, stopping once we're a few feet away. "I was hoping to catch you at work, actually."

"That was my intention as well." I shut my car door and look up to meet his eyes. He looks hurt and I hate it. "I'm sorry. I never meant to . . ."

"It's not your fault." He shakes his head, before running his hands down his bruised face. "It's our fault. Mine and Jameson's. We were assholes for letting you get involved. And it pisses me off that it's probably my fault the most."

"Why?" I lean against my car and watch as he shoves his hands into his pockets.

He looks embarrassed to be telling me whatever it is he's about to say. "I slept with his girlfriend of four years. I didn't do it for my pleasure. I did it to open his eyes and make a point to him that Katie had been sleeping around behind his back and lying."

He stops talking and nervously runs his hands through his hair. "I knew catching her with me would be all the proof he needed. I was an asshole and didn't think it through enough. And *that's* why you and Jameson ended up together. He wanted to make me work for you." He shakes his head and huffs. "It worked and fighting for you ended up not being enough."

I seriously have no idea what to say to what he just told me, so I just nod my head and look out toward the cornfield. Jameson mentioned Cole sleeping with his girlfriend, but we didn't get into the details of the whole story.

"I'm not mad at you, Brooke."

I turn my head to look at him, when I feel him step up beside me. "But you're mad at Jameson?"

"Yeah." He steps in close and places his hand on my chin. "I hate him right now, but it's not the first time I've felt like killing him. Hasn't happened yet." His body moves in closer as his eyes meet mine. "Are you happy?"

His closeness has me feeling uneasy so I turn away and begin talking quickly. "Yes. I haven't been this happy for a long time," I admit. "I care about him a lot, Cole. I feel good being with him. I . . ."

"Good." He releases my chin and smiles. "I'm glad to hear you're happy, Brooke. I think that's what matters the most to both of us. Doesn't mean it's going to be easy to forgive Jameson. The sight of him still pisses me off. But for you, I won't kill him."

The look on his face has me laughing. "Thank you, I think."

"I should get going before Jameson comes outside for a cigarette break and gets the impression I'm trying to pick you up." He points at his face. "This shit still hurts. I don't want to add to the misery. My face is too sexy to feel this bad."

We both laugh this time as Cole backs away and then turns

around to jump into his car.

I feel just a tad bit better, knowing Cole will be okay. I also have hope after our chat that with time, the boys will be on speaking terms again.

I stand here by my car, enjoying the fresh air for a few minutes, before I look over to see Jameson coming toward me.

Without hesitation, he picks me up in his arms and lifts my legs up to wrap around his waist.

All the uneasiness and stress I was just feeling from my conversation with Cole is completely gone, replaced by the warmth of being in Jameson's arms again.

I melt into his body, holding onto him tightly as he runs his scruffy face over my neck. "Fuck, I've been dying to see you all day, baby."

He kisses my neck and then moves his way up to roughly press his lips against mine, taking my damn breath away.

His kiss has me moaning and digging my fingertips into his strong shoulders. I don't think I'll ever be able to get enough of this man. "Same here," I breathe. "Work couldn't have gone by any slower tonight. I was losing my mind."

He walks us over so he can set me on the trunk of my car, keeping his body pressed between my legs. Not that I plan to let him go anytime soon. "I saw you and Cole talking." His thumb brushes over my bottom lip as he looks me in the eye, looking concerned for me. "Did he say anything disrespectful to you?"

I shake my head and gently run my fingers over his bruised face. It looks even worse than it did a few nights ago. I hate his beautiful face looking so painful. "No. I promise." I kiss his face all over, smiling when he grabs my face and holds it still.

"Come here," he demands.

Once he releases my face, I lean in and brush my lips over his, giving him a taste of what he wants. I'll always give him what he wants.

"Kiss me," he growls.

Wrapping my hands in his hair, I kiss him harder than I have in days. My heart skips a beat when I feel his perfect teeth nip my lip and pull roughly as if he wants to take me right here.

Jameson has a way of being sweet and dirty at the same time and I love it.

"Break over, Romeo." I hear a deep voice say through his earpiece.

I can't be sure, but it sounds like Rowdy.

"Remind me to choke Rowdy later for interrupting this perfect fucking moment." He growls against my lips, before pressing his hips into me, showing me just how hard he is. "My place or yours tonight?"

I wrap my legs tighter around him, not wanting to let go yet. I love the way his hard body feels between my legs. "Hmmm . . . your place. There's still a lot to set up at mine."

"I'll be there," he teases.

I laugh. "But don't be surprised if you walk in to find Karson crashed out on your couch. She wants to hang out for a while and watch some TV. That means she won't want to go home."

"Your friends are welcome at my place just as much as mine are." His muscles flex under my hands as he tangles his hands into the back of my hair and kisses me. "I'll be home in a few hours. Don't be surprised if I wake you up to pick up where we left off."

I unwrap my legs from around his waist and smile as he backs away, looking me up and down as if he wants to attack my body with his mouth. "Don't be surprised if I'm awake in your bed waiting, *Romeo*."

"Fuck," he says softly. "This is going to be the longest three hours of my life. I'll try to get off early."

I sit here on my car, smiling like a fool, for ten minutes after

Jameson is gone, before finally jumping in my car to meet Karson.

I feel an emptiness in my chest, the moment I pull out of the parking lot, heading away from Jameson.

That's exactly how I know that with each day I spend with him, I fall deeper and deeper into him. And this is only after spending six nights in a row with him.

I'm looking forward to seeing how this man can make me feel after a month . . .

EPILOGUE

One Month Later

Brooke

'M STANDING AT THE KITCHEN island, chopping up vegetables for dinner when I hear Jameson whistle from the doorway.

My entire body ignites with heat when I look over to see him gripping onto the doorframe, standing shirtless in a pair of low hanging sweats. His hard, tattooed body is still dripping wet from the shower he just took, making him look that much more desirable.

"It smells delicious in here." He lifts a brow and releases the doorframe. My eyes wander his glorious body, watching as his ab muscles flex when he speaks. "Thought it was my turn to cook dinner?"

I smile and fight to pull my eyes away from him so I can continue cooking. It's soooo hard. "You're distracting me. Go away before I cut a finger off."

Ignoring my demand, he comes up behind me and runs his

hands down my sides, while slowly kissing my neck. My body instantly melts into his, going crazy with need when I feel his erection press against my ass.

Everything with Jameson only seems to intensify the more I'm with him. Some days I can hardly even handle being in the same room with him without wanting his hands all over me as he takes me.

"What's distracting you?" He tilts my neck to the side and presses his entire body flush against my backside. The feel of his lips brushing up my neck as he makes his way to my ear, has me dropping the knife and closing my eyes. "My body?"

I nod my head, my breathing picking up when I feel his hands lower to my ass and squeeze.

"My hands?"

I nod my head again, biting my bottom lip when I feel his hands move to lift my skirt up. My breath escapes me, causing me to reach back and grip his hair when I feel him slide into me from behind, stopping once he fills me.

"My cock?"

"Mmm . . . Jameson . . ." I lean my head back and grab his hair with both hands now, moaning as he slowly thrusts in and out of me.

His hands run across my body, his mouth kissing me in ways only he can make me melt, as he continues to take me slow and deep, showing me just how passionate he can be when it comes to me.

"I'll always take care of your body, Brooke," he breathes into my neck, before kissing it again. "I'll never grow tired of making *love* to you and hearing you whimper my name as you come for me."

My heart speeds up at the mention of the word *love*. I've completely fallen head over heels in love with Jameson, but I haven't had the courage to say it first.

Even just hearing him say he's making love to me has my heart doing flips and my stomach filling with butterflies.

"You're the *only* one I want making love to me, Jameson."

My words cause his movements to freeze and his breathing to pick up against my neck as if my words affected him just as much as his did me.

"Good," he breathes out, before tilting my chin back so his lips are brushing against mine. "Because I *love* you. I'm in fucking *love* with you and it's driving me crazy to ever think of another man being inside you."

My heart stops from his confession and I'm overwhelmed with emotions, almost making me completely lose it in his arms.

I wait until I'm able to catch my breath, before I roughly pull his mouth against mine and speak against them. "I love you, too. So fucking much. I have for a while now and it's all I've been able to think about."

His mouth captures mine with a desperation I've never felt from him before as he begins moving inside of me again, catching each of my moans with his mouth.

The way he moves inside me feels different than the other times. It *feels* as if he's trying to show me how much he loves with me with each time he enters me.

Within a few minutes, I'm crying out his name, as he fills me, us both coming undone at the same time.

His strong arms hold me tightly, as we breath heavily against each other's mouth, slowly recovering from our high.

"Fuck, I've been going crazy to tell you that for a while and hear it back from you." I feel him smile against my neck, before he kisses it. "Best moment of my damn life, hearing those words leave your lips. No lie."

I laugh and pull him down by his neck so I can kiss him again. "I've been going just as crazy to hear it. You have no idea."

He moves around to kiss the back of my neck, before pulling out of me and reaching to pull his sweats back up. "Why don't you go shower and I'll finish dinner like I'm supposed to."

"But, I've already started it . . ."

Before I can finish what I'm saying, he picks me up and throws me over his shoulder, stalking toward the bathroom with a growl.

Once inside he sets me down and turns on the water, before undressing me. *"I'll* finish dinner. You just shower and get ready for tonight. My little sister's mean as shit. She'll kick my ass if I'm late for her welcoming back party."

I laugh as he grabs me by the hips all alpha like and sets me down in the shower. "Keep handling me all rough like this and we might not make it to the party." I smirk as he looks my body over, his chest quickly rising and falling.

He steps into the shower, sweats and all and roughly kisses me, under the water, knocking my breath out from the impact. *"Fuck,* I love you so much."

I grab onto his shoulders, digging my nails in as he picks me up and presses me against the wall. "You have no idea how much I love hearing those words come from your mouth."

His body grinds against mine, causing me to get lost in the moment, before I finally push my way out of his arms and smile against his chest. "As much as I'm dying for you to take me *again*, I don't want your sister kicking your ass. Especially if she's as mean as you say."

"Damn this fucking party." He looks as if he's fighting the urge to bend me over, before he finally steps out of the shower, removes his wet sweats and reaches for a towel. "Dinner will be ready in fifteen."

After he leaves, I fall against the shower wall, fighting to catch my breath.

The way this man makes me feel is unlike anything I've ever

experienced in my entire life. It's raw, passionate and breathtaking.

I love Jameson so much it almost hurts.

I never thought I'd experience a love so wild and intense that would just grow with every day we're together, but I was wrong.

So damn wrong.

He's captured my heart completely and I hope with everything in me he never gives is back . . .

Jameson

I ABOUT LOST MY SHIT when Brooke told me she loved me back, earlier.

Every day with her only seems to have my ass falling further in love with her, needing her in my arms and my life more and more. This woman is enough to bring me to my fucking knees.

She has a way of making me feel things no one has ever been able to make me feel. I'm completely, madly fucking in love with her.

Just the thought of her being in another man's arms kills me. I plan to do everything in my power to make sure that shit never happens and from what she shows me, I have nothing to worry about.

She's where she belongs now: with me. It wasn't easy getting her there, but now that she is, I'm sure as hell not letting her go.

Not even hurting my best friend was enough to keep me away from her. I'd hate to see anyone else try.

All the assholes in this room can look all they want, but touching what is *mine* will lead to someone getting thrown out the door by their fucking throat.

I don't care it's my night off.

I'm a reckless asshole when it comes to the woman I love and I will always protect her.

Taking care of her and making sure she feels loved is my top priority. *Always.*

I'm a lucky bastard for being the one that gets to keep her.

A confident smile crosses my face as I look across the room to see Brooke dancing with Karson and my sister Kai.

All the men in this room and I'm the one she can't take her eyes off. Makes me love her that much damn more.

I hear Rowdy talking beside me, but I'm too distracted by Brooke motioning for me to join her on the dancefloor, to pay attention to what he's saying.

He's so high right now that I haven't been able to get him to stop talking since we arrived over an hour ago.

I told myself I'd stay away from the dancefloor tonight, but Brooke looks too damn sexy in her little blue dress, making it impossible for me to refuse her request.

She knows it too, because I hear her laugh when I come up behind her and wrap my arms around her body. "Thought you weren't going to dance tonight?" she says teasingly.

I bite her neck and growl into her ear, causing her body to shiver in my arms. I've just recently discovered how much she loves the vibration of my growl against her ear, so I've been using it to make her weak any chance I get. "Only because I don't want to be sporting a hard-on with my sister in the damn room. You're making it impossible to avoid though. I'm already fucking hard and I've barely touched you."

"That's so gross." I look beside us when I hear my sister's disgusted voice. "I *really* didn't want to hear that coming from your mouth, Jameson. I've just moved back home after four years and this is what I have to listen to when I come back."

"I was hoping you're still into tuning me out like you used to when we were kids."

Brooke laughs and grabs for the drink Kai holds out to her. "Sorry. Your brother doesn't have much control over his dirty mouth."

"You're telling me," Karson says from over Kai's shoulder. "Try crashing out on the couch. You'll hear a lot of shit then. Keeps me up all night."

Kai's nose scrunches up as she makes a weird face. "Thanks for the warning. I don't think I'll take up that offer to sleep at your place until I find something."

"Like hell you aren't. My place is your place. I'm barely there anymore anyway. You're staying."

"And this is why I love you, big brother." Kai leans in and gives me a quick kiss on the cheek. "I've missed the hell out of you. So happy to be back."

"Hey, don't act like I never came to visit. You're the one that stayed away for so long."

My sister begins coming up with excuses that I just laugh at and turn away from.

Karson opens her mouth as if she's got something to say, but is quickly distracted by Rowdy squeezing his way in between us and dancing against her.

I laugh as Rowdy winks back at me and then dips Karson, surprising her. She looks completely lost in him, which has Brooke smiling into my shoulder.

Focusing back on Brooke, I move my body to the slow rhythm, placing my hands on her hips as she moves her body with mine.

Everything else in the room seems to fade out when she's near. All that exists is her and I love it.

I barely even notice Cole join the little party, until I look beside us to see him checking out my little sister. He's stopped by a few times to talk to us since we've arrived, but until now, he was held back by being on the clock.

Apparently, he's done for the night and has his eye on something he wants.

A growl escapes my throat when he tosses his drink back and moves in to dance against my sister.

The overwhelming feeling to choke him out takes over, but Brooke grabs my face, pulling it for me to look at her instead.

"Woah, killer. You and Cole are just getting things back to good." She stands up on her tippy toes and kisses me. "I'm sure he'll be respectful when it comes to Kai. They're just dancing. Give him a chance."

Cole better hope that's all he plans on doing with Kai. There's no way I'm letting that playboy get any closer to her than he is right now on the dancefloor.

He's just lucky Brooke is around to calm me down or I'd be throwing him across the room right about now.

"You *are* pretty sexy when you're all protective though," Brooke says against my neck. "I love that you're wanting to be a good brother and look out for Kai. Just another reason to love you more."

Her words calm me down, allowing me to get wrapped up in her and forget about Cole dancing with my sister.

It's when I see my sister walk away with Cole following behind her that I get pissed. That's never a good sight to see. Either she's trying to get away from him or *he's* trying to get into her pants.

Not fucking happening.

He's just about to catch up to her, when I grab him by the shirt and slam him against the wall. "The same rules still apply when it comes to my sister, motherfucker. Leave her alone."

Standing tall, he pushes me out of his face and grins. "Maybe those rules stopped mattering the second you took my girl." He playfully slaps my cheek and walks away, knowing damn well what he's getting myself into with this.

We might be on speaking terms again, but doesn't mean I won't kick his ass if I need to.

Damn Cole . . .

I swear he has the ability to piss me off more than anyone else I've ever met.

I start to relax when I feel Brooke's arms wrap around me from behind. "Your sisters up at the bar, talking with Karson and Violet. Come dance with me and *maybe* I'll let you take me home with you tonight."

Her words have me spinning around and picking her up. I slide my free hand behind her neck and pull her forehead against mine. "You always know the right thing to say to calm me down."

She smirks and leans in to kiss me. "That's why I get to keep you and no one else does."

I nod my head and suck her bottom lip into my mouth, before kissing her. All my worries seem to fade when I feel her tongue come out and swipe across my lips. "And it's exactly why you get my love too. That and many other reasons."

She squeezes me with her legs and presses her lips all over my face, like I do to her when I'm trying to cheer her up. "I love you, Jameson."

"Damn, baby." I set Brooke down and cup her face, before kissing her long and hard, showing everyone in this club how much she means to me. "I love you too."

And I plan to for a long fucking time. I'm not going anywhere . . .

THE END

ACKNOWLEDGEMENTS

FIRST AND FOREMOST, I'D LIKE to say a big thank you to all of my loyal readers that have given me support over the last few years and have encouraged me to continue with my writing. Your words have all inspired me to do what I enjoy and love. Each and every one of you mean a lot to me and I wouldn't be where I am if it weren't for your support and kind words.

I'd also like to thank my beta readers. I love you ladies and appreciate you taking the time to read my words. You know who you are! And Lindsey! Oh my goodness, lady. You helped me more than you can ever know! Thank you so much.

My amazingly, wonderful PA, Amy Preston Rogers. Her support has meant so much to me.

I'd like to thank another friend of mine, Clarise Tan from *CT Cover Creations* for creating my cover. You've been wonderful to work with and have helped me in so many ways.

Thank you to my boyfriend, friends and family for understanding my busy schedule and being there to support me through the hardest part. I know it's hard on everyone, and everyone's support means the world to me.

Last but not least, I'd like to thank all of the wonderful book bloggers that have taken the time to support my book and help spread the word. You all do so much for us authors and it is greatly appreciated. I have met so many friends on the way and you guys are never forgotten. You guys rock. Thank you!

ABOUT THE AUTHOR

VICTORIA ASHLEY GREW UP IN Rockford, IL and has had a passion for reading for as long as she can remember. After finding a reading app where it allowed readers to upload their own stories, she gave it a shot and writing became her passion.

She lives for a good romance book with tattooed bad boys that are just highly misunderstood and is not afraid to be caught crying during a good read. When she's not reading or writing about bad boys, you can find her watching her favorite shows such as Supernatural, Sons Of Anarchy, Game Of Thrones and The Walking Dead.

CONTACT HER AT:

www.victoriaashleyauthor.com

Facebook

Twitter: @VictoriaAauthor

Intstagram: VictoriaAshley.Author

BOOKS BY VICTORIA ASHLEY

Walk of Shame Series
Slade (Book 1)
Hemy (Book 2)
Cale (Book 3)

Walk of Shame 2nd Generation Series
Stone (Book 1)
Styx (Book 2)

Savage & Ink Series
Royal Savage (Book 1)

The Pain Series
Get Off On the Pain (Book 1)
Something For the Pain (Book 2)

STAND ALONE TITLES
Wake Up Call
This Regret
Thrust

BOOKS CO-WRITTEN WITH HILARY STORM
Alphachat.com Series
Pay For Play (Book 1)
Two Can Play (Book 2)